Sisters in Love

Snow Sisters, Book One

Love in Bloom Series

Melissa Foster

"A beautiful story about love and self-growth and finding
that balance to happiness. Powerfully written and
riveting from beginning to end."
-- *National bestselling author, Jane Porter*

ISBN-13: 978-0989050852
ISBN-10: 0989050858

SISTERS IN LOVE

Cover Design: Regina Starace

WORLD LITERARY PRESS
PRINTED IN THE UNITED STATES OF AMERICA

A NOTE TO MY READERS

When I first began writing Danica's and Kaylie's story, I felt like I'd met a group of new friends, and I knew that they were too special to let go after just one book. In book three of the *Snow Sisters* you will begin to meet the Bradens, a family of six hot, wealthy, and lovable siblings. The Bradens will be joining the Snow sisters in this light, fun, and sexy series—*Love in Bloom*—and I hope you fall in love with Danica, Blake, Kaylie, Chaz, the Braden siblings, and all of their friends, just as I have.

Melissa Foster

PRAISE FOR MELISSA FOSTER

"HAVE NO SHAME is a powerful testimony to love and the progressive, logical evolution of social consciousness, with an outcome that readers will find engrossing, unexpected, and ultimately eye-opening."
Midwest Book Review

"TRACES OF KARA is psychological suspense at its best, weaving a tight-knit plot, unrelenting action, and tense moments that don't let up, and ending in a fiery, unpredictable revelation."
Midwest Book Review

"[MEGAN'S WAY] A wonderful, warm, and thought-provoking story...a deep and moving book that speaks to men as well as women, and I urge you all to put it on your reading list."
Mensa Bulletin

"CHASING AMANDA – the MUST READ THRILLER OF 2011. Intelligent, entrancing, luminous."
Author Dean Mayes

"COME BACK TO ME is a hauntingly beautiful love story set against the backdrop of betrayal in a broken world."
Bestselling Author, Sue Harrison

For my husband, who understands when I fall in love
with my fictional characters

Chapter One

The line in the café went all the way to the door. Danica Snow wished she hadn't taken her sister Kaylie's phone call before getting her morning coffee. Living in an overcrowded tourist town could be a major inconvenience, but Danica loved that she could walk from her condo to her office, see a movie, have dinner, or even stop at a bookstore without ever sitting in a car. Every minute counted when you lived in Allure, Colorado, host to an odd mix of hippie and yuppie tourists in equal numbers. The ski slopes brought them in the winter, while art shows drew them in the summer. There was never a break. Every suit and Rasta child in town was standing right in front of her, waiting for their coffee or latte, and the guy ahead of her had shoulders so wide she couldn't easily see around him. Danica tapped the toe of her efficient and comfortable Nine West heels, growing more impatient by the second.

What on earth was taking so long? In seven minutes they'd served only one person. The tables were pushed so close to the people standing in line that she couldn't step to the side to see. She was gridlocked. Danica leaned to the right and peered around the massive shoulder ahead of her just as the owner of that shoulder turned to look out the door. *Whack!* He elbowed her right in the nose, knocking Danica's head back.

Her hand flew to her bloody nose. "Ow! Geez!" She ducked in pain, covering her face and talking through her hands. "I think you broke my nose." Each word sent pain across her nose and below her eyes.

"I'm so sorry. Let me get you a napkin," a deep, worried voice said.

Two patrons rushed over and shoved napkins in her direction.

"Are you okay?" an older woman asked.

Tears sprang from the corners of Danica's closed eyes. *Damn it.* Her entire day would now run late and she probably looked like a red-nosed, crying idiot. "This hurts so bad. Weren't you looking where—" Danica flipped her unruly, brown hair from her face and opened her eyes. Her venom-filled glare locked on the man who had elbowed her—the most beautiful specimen of a human being she had ever seen. *Oh shit.* "I'm...What...?" *Come on, girl. Get it together. He's probably an egomaniac.*

"I'm so sorry." His voice was rich and smooth, laden with concern.

2

A thin blonde grabbed his arm and shoved a napkin into his hand. "Give this to her," she said, blinking her eyelashes in a come-hither way.

The man held the woman's hand a beat too long. "Thanks," he said. His eyes trailed down the blonde's blouse.

Really? I'm bleeding over here.

He turned toward Danica and handed her the napkin. His eyes were green and yellow, like field grass. His eyebrows drew together in a serious gaze, and Danica thought that maybe she'd been too quick to judge—until he stole a glance at the blonde as she walked out of the café.

Asshole. She felt the heat of anger spread up her chest and neck, along her cheeks, to the ridge of her high cheekbones. She snagged the napkin from his hand and wiped her throbbing nose. "It's okay. I'm fine," she lied. She could smell the minty freshness of his breath, and she wondered what it might taste like. Danica was not one to swoon—that was Kaylie's job. *Get a grip.*

"Can I at least buy you a coffee?" He ran his hand through his thick, dark hair.

Yes! "No, thank you. It's okay." She had been a therapist long enough to know what kind of guy eyes another girl while she was tending to a bloody nose that he had caused. Danica fumbled for her purse, which she'd dropped when she was hit. She lowered her eyes to avoid looking into his. "I'm fine, really. Just look behind you next time." Not for the first time, Danica wished she

3

had Kaylie's flirting skills and her ability to look past his wandering eyes. She would have had him buying her coffee, a Danish, and breakfast the next morning.

Danica was so confused, she wasn't even sure what she wanted. She chanced another glance up at him. He was looking at her features so intently that she felt as though he were drinking her in, memorizing her. His eyes trailed slowly from hers, lowered to her nose, to her lips, and then settled on the beauty mark that she'd been self-conscious of her entire life. She felt like a Cindy Crawford wannabe. Danica pursed her lips. "Are you done?" she asked.

He blinked with the innocence of a young boy, clueless to her annoyance, which was in stark contrast to his confident, manly presence. He stood almost a foot taller than Danica's impressive five foot seven stature. His chest muscles bulged beneath his way-too-small shirt, dark curls poking through the neckline. *He probably bought it that way on purpose.* She glanced down and tried not to notice his muscular thighs straining against his stonewashed denim jeans. Danica swallowed hard. All the air suddenly left her lungs. He was touching her shoulder, squinting, evaluating her face.

"I'm sorry. I was just making sure it didn't look broken, which it doesn't. I'm sure it's painful."

She couldn't think past the heat of his hand, the breadth of it engulfing her shoulder. "It's okay," she managed, hating herself for being lost in his touch when he was clearly someone who ate women for breakfast. She checked her watch. She had three minutes to get her coffee and get back to her office before her next client showed up. *Belinda. She'd love this guy.*

The line progressed, and Adonis waved as he left the café. Danica reached into her purse to pay for her French vanilla coffee and found herself taking a last glance at him as he passed the front window.

The young barista pushed Danica's money away. "No need, hon. Blake paid for yours." She smiled, lifting her eyebrows.

"He did?" *Blake.*

"Yeah, he's really sweet." The barista leaned over the cash register. "Even if he is a player."

Aha! I knew it. Danica thrust her shoulders back, feeling smart for resisting temptation.

Chapter Two

Danica sat across from Belinda Trenton, desperately trying to focus on her client's latest issue instead of the pain she felt every time she sniffled or blinked. It hurt, but her nose hadn't blossomed into a swollen mess, so she was pretty sure it wasn't broken. Belinda chewed gum like a cow chews its cud. Her eyeliner was reminiscent of Madonna's style from the eighties. Her dark hair was long and thick, pinned up in the very front with a petite barrette, leaving sexy tendrils hanging past her silver-rimmed glasses. She looked like a vixen librarian. The tops of her breasts plumped out of the low-cut T-shirt she wore, and her black skinny jeans looked more like a second skin than a layer of clothing. She bounced her stiletto heels as she spoke. *Blake would love you*, Danica thought, before quickly chiding herself for being snarky.

"I wasn't going to sleep with him. I really wasn't," Belinda said, continuing her rationale for her previous evening's romp.

"I'm not here to judge you, Belinda. It's okay if you did want to sleep with him. But I thought you were trying to restrain yourself. Trying a new tactic." Same conversation, different day. Belinda was no more in charge of her hormones than the sky had the power to withhold rain. Danica's thoughts turned to Blake's shoulders, and she wondered what it might feel like to touch them. *Oh God, what's happening to me?* If even she couldn't keep her thoughts focused—and she was the least sexual person she knew—how could she expect her sexed-up clients to?

"I know. I was. Meet them, chat, and don't take them home, right?" Belinda looked at her for affirmation.

"Yes." She mulled over what Belinda had done. What was so bad about it, really? She was attracted to a man and went home with him. Ever since that morning, all Danica could think about was what would have happened if she'd let Blake buy her coffee. For the first time in her life, Danica was wondering about that moment of impact, that instant attraction that so many could not deny—her sister included. She wondered why Kaylie had that level of desire and why she didn't. She'd always thought that she was the less troubled one. Now, after experiencing heart-pounding excitement at the sight of Blake, she began to wonder if something was wrong with her after all. Why hadn't she ever felt this way before?

"Well, I tried that, but he just kept offering. He said he had this great, new CD he wanted me to hear—and I like music."

I like coffee. "Do you know what you're doing?"

Belinda rolled her eyes. "Rationalizing."

Danica nodded. Some people would call Belinda a sex addict. Even Danica had lost track of the number of men that had shared Belinda's bed in the past year. But Danica didn't like that term—sex addict. She felt it was a cop out. Being promiscuous was something that seemed to drive Belinda from one moment to the next, and Danica knew that when Belinda discovered more about herself and gained more confidence, the need for meaningless sex would wane.

She didn't mean to, but she knew she was giving Belinda the disapproving parental look that she herself despised. Strangely, she felt the look was meant more for herself than Belinda. How many times had her father given her that same look for doing something whimsical instead of academic, while praising Kaylie for her song and dance routines? She pictured him now with his thick, dark hair, one bushy eyebrow lifted, as if to say, *Don't waste your time on that silliness.* She pictured her proper mother, demure with her blunt-cut hair and ever-present smile. She didn't have to say a word to Danica about her behavior. The way she'd nodded in support of her father was enough to send a strong message: Danica was the smart one. Her father's voice still rang out in her mind, *There are certain expectations we have of you that we simply cannot expect of Kaylie.*

Time to wrap this session up.

"Okay, so, next week we'll work on learning the downfalls of rationalizing your actions away." *And, hopefully, I'll be able to think past the sexy man who gave me a bloody nose.*

Belinda bit her lower lip and stood eye to eye with Danica. "Do you think there's hope for me? Or am I always going to be like this?" Her eyes pleaded for help or some sort of kudos, something to validate that she wasn't looking at a mountain that she could never climb.

Danica knew the power of positive thinking. She patted Belinda on the back and said, "You can do anything you're really determined to do, Belinda. We just need to work on some of these things. I have faith in you." *Validation on a paper plate. Why am I such a magnet for promiscuous people?* She thought about it, then silently added, *Even my sister!*

Chapter Three

Blake Carter listened to the two cougars whispering about him from behind the ski rack. He eyed them as he walked toward the front of the store. The dark-haired one looked vaguely familiar. The redhead flashed him a smile as he walked past. He gave her his best over-the-shoulder glance, holding her gaze. *Nice rack, nice ass.* He busied himself behind the counter, counting up the receipts, glancing up when they giggled like schoolgirls. He was playing a game, doing what he knew best. But ever since that woman he'd hurt in the coffee shop noticed him taking a last glance at the slinky blonde, he had actually felt bad. He'd seen the hurt in the woman's eyes as she stood there with blood on her nose, and it was like his heart had softened. Ever since that moment, those hurt eyes lingered in his mind, and now he was having trouble seeing past them.

"They're hot for you."

Blake lifted his eyes to Dave Tuft, his best friend, business partner, and the best acroskier he knew. Dave could flip and spin on a pair of skis as well as Blake could land women.

"What else is new?"

Dave shook his head. "So, you goin' for it?" He lifted his eyebrows.

"No, thanks." Blake laughed, wishing the woman from the café had accepted his offer to buy her a cup of coffee. He could have made up for the sneak peek at the blonde.

"You can't handle two?" Dave pulled an inventory clipboard from below the counter and glanced over at the fifty-something-year-old women. "I envy you, but I wouldn't trade Sally or Rusty for anyone in the world."

"Just wait. Rusty's what? Fifteen? Soon he'll be doing what I'm doing, if he's not already."

"Maybe, but we spend so much family time together that I can't even imagine it."

"Tell me about it. When are we hitting the slopes again? Between Rusty's basketball and your weekly date night with Sally, we never get to catch air together. We should take a run, let our Kodak courage run wild." Blake knew from experience that if he egged him on enough, Dave would eventually relent. Dave's commitment to Sally and Rusty was enviable, but Blake missed their skiing excursions.

"Kodak courage, huh?" Dave laughed. "I think it takes Kodak courage to do what you do." He nodded at the women. "I'm too old and too tired to show *that* kind of courage."

Dave was five years older than Blake, and at thirty-four, Blake still couldn't imagine being too tired for sex. He turned away from the women and leaned against the counter. He couldn't get the woman from the café off his mind. She was bitchy and cold and had made it very clear that she was too good for him when she snubbed his offer to buy her coffee, and yet, when he'd looked into her eyes, he'd been intrigued by some kind of repressed spark. Maybe it was just the old adage: *Everyone wants what they can't have.* All he knew was that for the first time in years, he had no stirrings for the women who were so eagerly vying for his attention, and he was pissed at having been blown off earlier.

"As much as I egg you on, dude, I gotta tell ya, life is complicated enough. One woman—the right woman—is more than enough for me. I have to wonder why on earth you're so afraid of getting married," Dave said.

"Not afraid. Too smart to get caged." Blake smiled. "Come on. Whaddaya say? One more ski trip before the season's over?"

"You know, there are people who can help you work through that mommy drama of yours." Dave pulled out his cell phone scrolled through his contacts. He scribbled a number on a piece of paper, then shoved it into Blake's pants' pocket. "I looked her up a few months ago. I didn't see her, but I heard she's great."

"Hooker?"

"Therapist," Dave said with a serious tone. "Okay, look, it *has* been a while since we've skied. Rusty has a game tomorrow, but how about a night run on Saturday?"

Blake eyed Dave expectantly, waiting for him to say that he forgot he had plans with Sally, Rusty needed help studying, or it was family movie night at their house. He touched his pocket, wondering why Dave would have a therapist's number, then dismissed the thought and moved on to planning their evening of skiing.

"What?" Dave asked.

"Hadn't you better check with wifey first?" Blake asked.

"Sally doesn't care what I do. I mean, she cares, but it's my choice."

Blake heard hesitation in Dave's voice and raised his eyebrows.

"I know you can't understand this, Casanova, but I actually like spending time with my family. I like the mundane of knowing they're there. I like coming home to the same woman every day, knowing what perfume she'll have on, and yes, even knowing that Friday nights are family movie night and Sundays are our date night." Dave sighed. "Look, Saturday night. I'll make it happen."

Blake shook his head.

"What's that? Blood?" Dave pointed to Blake's elbow.

"What?" Blake looked at a smear of blood on his elbow. "Goddamnit." He walked toward the bathroom to wash it off. Now the snarky woman had ruined his favorite Rossignol long-sleeve shirt. Sure, he had too many of the same type of shirt from every manufacturer around, but this shirt was the one his father had mailed him when they'd opened their ski shop, AcroSki. It was light gray, one size too small, and hugged him in all the right places. The perfect base layer. It was his lucky shirt, and now it was probably ruined.

Dave was on his heels. "Blood? What's up with that?"

"I elbowed some woman by accident at the coffee shop. She got a bloody nose." The woman he couldn't get out of his mind, with the cutest mole he'd ever seen right above her luscious lips.

"Is that why you're in a shitty mood?" Dave asked.

Blake stopped walking and turned to face Dave. "I'm not in a shitty mood. I'm just tired."

"If this isn't a shitty mood, then you're a virgin, too."

Blake pressed his lips into a tight line and walked away.

The bathroom was bright and, thankfully, empty. Blake pulled at his shirtsleeve to inspect the damage. He'd never hit a woman before, not even by accident, and the one time he made a mistake, she bleeds all over his favorite shirt? Just his luck. He pulled his shirt over his head and rinsed the elbow area with cold water. The water turned pink from the runoff.

The bathroom door swung open, the *Men's Room* sign clear in big, bold, blue letters on the door.

"Oops. Sorry," the redhead said with a coy smile.

15

Blake feigned a smile in return. He was in no mood for a quick bathroom romp. He'd done it before— bathroom, airplane, even on a ski lift. Hell, there was probably nothing he hadn't done before, but he was not in the mood for it now.

The woman shimmied over and put her hand on his bare back. "Want some help with that?" She leaned in close, brushed her breast against his bare chest.

Blake steeled his stance. "I've got it, thanks."

Red reached over and put her hands on top of his, moving it in a scrubbing motion just as he was. "I'm good with my hands. I can probably get that right out."

I'll bet you are. Her hair smelled of roses, her shoulder and neck of Obsession perfume. Blake felt the familiar desire pulling him toward her. He leaned back. *Behave*, he told himself, but his body had other ideas.

The woman turned and put her wet hands on Blake's biceps, her lips an inch from his. "My girlfriend," she said, running her wet index finger down his arm, "said you liked a little fun."

"Did she?" Blake had a hazy recollection of the other woman from the only non-touristy bar in town, Bar None. He cringed. Was the town really that small? Blake was torn between his growing erection and the anger he'd felt moments before she'd come into the bathroom.

"Mm-hmm. I thought I might meet you after work and," she leaned in and whispered in his ear, "help you release some stress. Drinks, my place?" She planted soft kisses down his neck.

To any other man, this might have seemed unusual, but to Blake—who'd been intimate with too many women to count, in too many places to remember—this was an everyday occurrence. Something he normally thrived on. Today, all he wanted was to clean his damned shirt and forget the woman from earlier that morning.

Her lips moved down his chest, circling his nipple.

"You look stressed. Maybe this will help." She ran her tongue down his stomach and back up again.

Blake dropped his shirt into the sink and turned, pressing his groin into the woman's hips. "Maybe it would." Unable to withstand the sizzling heat of her lust, he gave in to the familiar release that he'd given in to over a hundred times before. He brought his lips to her neck, kissing and licking until she was moaning, grabbing his ass and pulling it toward her. His eyes lingered on the shirt. His favorite shirt. The shirt that was stained with that other woman's blood. His erection faltered.

Red reached for his crotch, massaging him through his jeans, and planted quick licks of her tongue on his neck and chest. The wetness lingered there, cool and sharp. She unbuttoned his jeans, the tip of his erection pressed against the waistband of his black Calvin Klein boxer briefs. She slid her hand inside the denim and cradled his balls through the soft cotton.

Blake closed his eyes, submitting to the desire that swelled within him. *Not good enough for you?* Anger at the morning's snub surged through him. *I'll show you how good I am.* He grabbed Red by the back of her head and kissed her hard. She moaned with pleasure, her hand still working its magic. He lifted her up and onto the counter, forcefully reaching under her dress and pulling her thong to the side. He pushed his pants down, slipped on a condom, and wrapped her legs around his waist. She pulled away from his grasp, looking down at his massive erection.

"Oh yeah, she wasn't lying," she purred. She pulled him against her.

With one hand, he grabbed her ass and lifted her forward, to the edge of the counter, the tip of his penis against her opening. She was wet, ready. With one thrust, he was inside of her. She gasped, digging her fingernails into his shoulders and sending his erection into overdrive. He pumped hard and fast. Her head fell back as she arched into him. He kissed her long neck, twisting out of her fingernails' grasp and driving even deeper. The snarky woman's voice invaded his thoughts. *Are you done?* Usually Blake waited for the woman to orgasm before finding his release. Today he had to escape his own thoughts. He thrust and pumped until he was on the verge of his own orgasm.

Red panted, "Wait. Wait. Go slower."

Are you done? There was no waiting. Anger fed his need. He clung to her ample hips as he pulled her forward and pushed her back in perfect rhythm with each of his harsh thrusts, until finally, she squeezed and pulsated around him and he came hard and forcefully, gritting his teeth and grunting against her neck until he was spent.

"Fun," she said, out of breath.

Blake opened his eyes to find his own reflection staring back at him in the mirror. His cheeks carried the pink of fresh desire and his lips were smeared with her lipstick. His jeans hung around his knees, and the fifty-something-year-old woman he'd just banged was hanging on to him like he was hers. He didn't even know her name. *Fun?* He was a thirty-four-year-old male slut—no better than those girls everyone teased in high school. *Are you done?* Her voice echoed in his head. Blake pulled out of Red, grabbed paper towels from the dispenser, and handed them to her. "Thanks," he said, tossing his condom in the trash. Then he snagged his shirt, hiked up his pants, and escaped with his shame and self-loathing to the safety of his office.

Chapter Four

Saturday evening the moon cast a foggy glow over the mountaintop. The slopes looked like fluffy clouds that had fallen to the ground. Blake inhaled the icy, wet smell of the slopes. He loved night skiing, when the slopes were filled with more experienced skiers.

"You ready, buddy?" Dave asked as he skied into place next to Blake. He stood six inches shorter but was every bit as thick and muscular as Blake. A light snow began to fall.

"Yeah, I'm ready. Listen, I feel kind of guilty taking you away from your family."

"No, you don't."

"Yeah." Blake smiled. "I don't."

They both laughed.

"I'm glad you came. It's been a month since we've hit the slopes."

"I know. You remind me every day." Dave raised an eyebrow. "No worries, man. I wouldn't miss it for the world. Time goes quick. All this powder will be gone before we know it."

"You could've brought Rusty if you wanted," Blake said.

"Yeah, just what you need, a teenager hanging around. No way, man. This run is just for us. I need the break, too. Besides, Rusty has as much interest in skiing as I do in basketball. He's a kid. He has the joy of picking and choosing his addictions."

They took the ski lift to the top of the second tallest trail. By the time they reached the peak, the snow was coming down hard. Adrenaline rushed through Blake as they stepped from the lift and skied to the crest. He and Dave wore similar Arc'teryx Stingray jackets and Völkl pants, compliments of their suppliers. Dave's were royal blue, and Blake wore black and red. Free clothing was just one of the many perks of owning a ski shop.

"I feel great tonight!" Dave said. The cold night's air was already turning his cheeks pink. He shielded his eyes from the falling snow with his gloved hand.

"I feel great every night," Blake said. "Damn, it's really coming down. Let's take the first one easy, warm up."

Dave's cell phone rang.

"You brought that damn thing with you? I love Sally, but come on." Blake really did love Sally, and the times he'd gotten together with Dave's family had always been enjoyable—barbeques, dinners out on the town, the fair every summer —but he would never want to be that accessible to anyone. He considered his ski time sacred.

Dave took out his phone. "Wifey calls." He held up one finger to Blake. "Hi, honey. Yeah, we made it. Yup, getting ready right now for our first run." He paused, listening to Sally. "Put him on." Dave turned his back, then spoke sternly into the phone. "Is what your mother said true? What the hell were you thinking?" Dave paced. "You listen to me. If I come home and—" He stopped walking. "Rusty? Hello? Hello!" He looked at his phone. "Damn it." He shoved the phone in his pocket and, as he made his way through the thick curtain of snow that fell around them, Blake noticed him stabbing his poles into the ground and the fine lines forming around his pinched face.

"Everything okay?" Blake asked.

"Lost connection," he snapped. "Goddamnit. You wouldn't understand. Let's just go."

"Okay, if you're sure." The last thing Blake wanted to do was listen to the details of an argument. He was itching to get onto the slopes.

"I'm takin' the back." Dave's breath came out in foggy huffs. He pulled his yellow goggles down over his eyes and turned away.

"Whoa, the back? Dave, come on. You know how this goes. Warm up. Then, when you're—" Blake watched Dave stomp, not ski, in the direction of the back side of the mountain. Visibility was already an issue. He pulled his goggles down over his eyes and opened his mouth to call to Dave, but he was nowhere in sight. "Meet you at the bottom," he said to himself.

Blake took the front side of the mountain slow and easy, relishing in the familiar whisking of the cold snow against his face. His knees knew just where and when to bend; his body took the turns with practiced memory. Reckless kids sped past him at racing speeds. He smiled. That's how he had been at that age, indestructible. *I still am*, he thought to himself with pride. He picked up speed. The snow was coming down thick and fast.

Blake wondered if he should have stopped Dave from skiing down the back of the mountain. It wasn't as well lit as the front, and that side of the mountain had steep cliffs and a rough terrain interspersed with trees and enormous moguls. He thought of Sally at home with their son while Dave was here having fun, and the way Dave had reacted to the phone call. Marriage was a strange equation to Blake. No matter how he added it up, one plus one did not equate to a lifetime of happiness and excitement. He wondered if he'd ever be content with just one woman in his life, if he'd ever be able to sleep with just one woman—or if he'd ever *want* to.

He slid into the clearing at the bottom of the hill and saw the rescue team suiting up. He had yet to ski at night without seeing an accident. The trails were filled with rookies who thought they could take a high bump and kids who knew no boundaries. There were five trails at the resort, and he'd skied them all. The back wasn't even the toughest terrain. There was one higher, rougher trail, accessible only by the ski lift that had dropped them at the crest of the trail. It also went all the way to the top, to the crest of Little Hellion. Only experienced skiers were allowed to ski Little Hellion, and they wore special tags on their jackets. Blake looked down at his tag. He and Dave had passed the course requirements for taking on Little Hellion three years earlier. He remembered that afternoon fondly. He and Dave had ribbed each other about the other one failing to tackle the pre-Hellion trails, but they both surpassed the expected skill level. Hot-dog Dave even flipped over a few of the moguls, angering the instructors. Blake smiled at the memory. When it came to skiing, Dave had always been a show-off.

The rescue team headed right while Blake skied to the left, toward the end of the back run, to meet Dave. One of the rescue team's snowmobiles was pulling out, and Blake skied off to the side to let it pass.

"Where's the fall?" he hollered.

"Little Hellion. Just closed the slope. Be careful out there." The snowmobile zoomed away at full throttle.

Blake knew that if the slope was closed, the accident was bad. He wondered who'd been dumb enough to ham it up on Little Hellion on a night like tonight.

The fresh powder made the trek toward the back take longer than it should. When Blake finally arrived, a handful of skiers were sliding into the unpacked snow, sending thick sheets of snow careening into the air. Blake stood off to the side and waited for Dave.

After fifteen minutes, he wondered if he'd missed Dave and if he'd already headed back up the lift for another run. As a twenty-something-year-old guy came to a stop at the bottom of the hill, Blake asked him if he'd seen Dave.

"He's about this tall." Blake held up his hand to eye level. "Royal-blue jacket, great skier."

"Nope. Dude, it's rough up there. I couldn't see ten feet in front of me, but I didn't see anyone stuck or hurt, if that's what you mean. I did hear of an accident up on Little Hellion."

"Right, thanks." Blake headed back toward the front of the mountain. When he reached the lift, he decided to wait a little longer. Dave had been upset. Maybe he just wanted to be alone for a while. Hell, he'd take one more quick trip down the mountain and then look for Dave. What could it hurt? Dave was a big boy.

The ski lift bumped over each of the pole junctions. The skiers below Blake became tiny specs amid a sea of white as he ascended the mountain. At the top, he skied off the lift and stood at the crest, admiring the magnificent view. Blake was five when he first began skiing with his father, and by the time he was seven, he was already catching air. As a teen, he'd joined a weekend ski team. The older kids hung out together before and after practice. They'd spent practically all day on Saturdays and Sundays on the slopes. What had started as a dare between friends—flip over the biggest mogul you can find—turned into a competition, then a passion, and later, into a full-blown obsession. From then on, Blake was hooked. He'd even taken private lessons and learned to acroski better than anyone he'd ever met, with the exception of Dave.

They'd met as adults, on the slopes. Dave had just finished a big jump; he'd spun off of a cliff, landed perfectly, and zoomed the rest of the way down the slope. Blake had complimented him. *Man, you sure hurled your carcass up there. Nice.* Dave said thanks, but walked away and totally blew him off. So Blake took to the cliff. He wasn't one to be ignored—or outdone. Dave acted like he wasn't watching, but Blake knew better. To be an acroskier you had to be competitive. After Blake's perfect, corked spin, Dave approached and offered to teach him how to straighten it out. It took a minute for Blake to realize that Dave was joking, and when he had, they'd become fast friends. Dave Tuft was a master. Truly gifted. He could catch more air, perform masterful flips, and twist in ways that Blake still couldn't replicate. Dave knew it, too, and at times that confidence made him reckless. He'd broken his fair share of bones.

A helicopter flew in low overhead. *This can't be good.* Blake watched it descend toward the Little Hellion run.

The snowmobile came down the mountain and pulled onto the crest where Blake stood.

"We're closing the slopes. Take your last run." It was the same rescue team member that Blake had seen at the bottom of the hill.

"That was fast. Bad one, huh?" he asked.

The man took off his goggles and looked at Blake with serious, dark eyes. "Nothing we could do. The guy didn't make it."

Blake had a sinking feeling in his stomach.

"Near as we can tell, the guy must've misjudged his direction. Landed in the trees along the edge of the first cliff. Broken neck on impact."

The hair on the back of Blake's neck stood on end. "Jesus. Was he tagged for the mountain?"

"Yeah, he was tagged. Guy was wearing Arc'teryx and Völkl. He wasn't a novice."

The world spun around him. Blake's body went numb. "Yellow goggles?"

"You've seen him before?"

Dave.

Chapter Five

Danica sat in front of her television set in her favorite baggy, blue sweatpants and T-shirt, reviewing Belinda Trenton's file. A typical Saturday night for Danica. Danica knew Belinda's story all too well. Daddy didn't pay enough attention to her. She reached out for sex, hoping for love, and couldn't figure out why she was treated poorly. She had to make sure she wasn't missing anything from their earlier sessions. She could help this girl; there was no doubt about it. It's what she did best—helping pull the insecure and needy up by their bootstraps and start anew, with some semblance of confidence and willpower.

When her cell phone rang, she set the file down on her perfectly organized coffee table and glanced at the time.

"Hi, Kay."

"What's up, sis?" Her younger sister, Kaylie, was far too chipper for eleven o'clock at night. "Wait. Don't tell me. You're sitting in your living room poring over client files to figure out how you can help some poor sap who can't get it up."

"I wish it were that easy," she answered, thinking of Belinda. "Viagra works wonders. Unfortunately, it's not what this client needs." Danica laughed. Her younger sister knew how to get her head out of the office.

"Yeah, you're tellin' me?" Kaylie laughed.

Danica rolled her eyes. She'd long ago stopped trying to help Kaylie figure out that she didn't need to sleep with any man who happened to strike her fancy. "Are you drunk?"

"Let's just say I'm not exactly sober. Camille and the girls are here. Can you meet us?"

Danica and Kaylie had grown up on the same block as Camille Rochester, who was getting married to Jeffrey Danber in a few short weeks. They had been inseparable as kids, but now Danica was a twenty-nine-year-old therapist, working from sunup to sundown; Camille, a year younger, was wrapped up in being a bride-to-be; and Kaylie was a twenty-seven-year-old singer who lived life like a pseudo rock star.

"It's late, and I'm comfy. Can't Camille take care of you?"

Kaylie sighed. "You know Camille. She's spent the last twenty years planning her wedding. It's finally her time to shine, and I'm so sick of talking about her

30

wedding, I could puke. So suck it up, put on something with a little cleavage, and meet me in twenty minutes. Please?"

"Cleavage?"

Kaylie laughed. "Yeah. You know those things that sit on your chest? Let them show a little. Jesus, Danica, it's like you hole yourself up in your office and condo so often, you don't even know how to live anymore."

Danica surveyed her cozy living room. "At least I have a condo."

"Shut up," Kaylie snapped. "It's the same as my apartment, but you have a big-ass mortgage."

"And no bitchy roommates. I have to meet Michelle tomorrow morning." Danica had been mentoring ninth grader Michelle Parce for the past six months through the Big Sister program. When she'd first moved back to Allure, she'd toyed with the idea of opening a recreational youth center, someplace safe where teens could gather and hang out without the constant barrage of commercialization like a mall. She'd even thrown around the idea of having free social services for teens—not exactly therapy, but an ear for listening. A sounding board. Instead, she'd fallen prey to her parents' pressure of becoming a therapist and following the conventional route, and her dreams had fallen further and further away. Spending time with Michelle recently had rekindled her thoughts. Michelle's mother, Nancy, was a recovering alcoholic, and Michelle lived with her grandmother. "I can't show up with a hangover."

"Whatever. Then don't drink too much. You'd better be here in fifteen minutes or I'm sending in the troops. We're at Bar None." Kaylie hung up the phone.

Danica rued the idea of getting dressed and going to a loud bar after a long week of emotionally draining clients, but sending in the troops meant all the girls would show up on her doorstep and there'd be no getting rid of them. They'd camp out until Sunday night. She forced herself off of her comfortable perch and headed upstairs.

Danica stepped out of the shower and wrapped a fluffy white towel around her body. She cleared the steam from the mirror and inspected her nose, which was no longer red. She squinted her eyes, scrunched her mouth, moved her lips from side to side. She puckered, as if to kiss someone, and felt a slight painful tug on the sides of her nose. Not that kissing was even a remote possibility with her severe lack of a social life. *Well, then, guess I'll be pain free tonight.*

She thought of the last time she'd even tried to look sexy—ages ago. The image of Adonis's muscular chest and thick hair came back to her, sending a shiver up her spine. She'd liked the way her body tingled when he'd spoken with a voice so sexy it practically caressed her. She thought of the way his jeans stretched tight over his thighs and that too-tight shirt. What did his shirt say? Rossington? Rossignol? Was that a band? Should she know? Was her sister right? Had she holed herself up so much that she was missing out on life? Maybe tonight she'd sex it up a bit. Maybe tonight she'd just play with letting herself be open to seeing men the way Kaylie and Belinda did.

She used the diffuser to dry her hair, silently praying for a sexy outcome. She flipped her head upside down and held the dryer like a gun, shooting hot air through her thick mass of hair. *Please don't frizz.* With one swift flip of her head, her hair fell like a long, wild Afro around her head. Tiny ringlets sprang out in every direction. She groaned and threw the dryer onto the counter. *Hopeless.* She headed out of the bathroom.

Danica stood in her closet, staring at the black, silk, knee-length dress she'd worn to her friend's engagement party last year, then groaned. There was no way her extra ten pounds would fit into it. She'd been working so hard that she never even exercised anymore. Danica's closet was separated by style and weight. She passed the slinky, skinny section, which she fit into only under complete duress, when her body was so stressed that she couldn't eat—like when her mother visited. After Danica and Kaylie had graduated from college, their mother had moved to a small house just outside of the town limits—away from the memories of her failed marriage. With Danica's busy schedule, she didn't see her mother very often, and sometimes she wondered if her mother was lonely. Unfortunately, when they did get together, Danica still felt pressure to be the smart, responsible daughter, fielding her mother's questions about the potential husbands and grandchildren she so desired; the pressure never seemed to let up, making the prospect of visiting more often even less appealing.

She glanced at her work outfits, suits and professional dresses, and immediately nixed them. "Cleavage, cleavage," she whispered. She eyed the safe section of her closet. The safe section held the dresses and skirts that fit her no matter how thin or heavy she was and hid her muffin top well. She pulled a dark green, thigh-length dress from the safe section and held it against her towel, looking in the floor-length mirror. *Cleavage, check.* It had a nice wrap style that helped add a waist to her no longer slim figure. *Camouflage.*

With a coy smile, she snagged the only pair of Jimmy Choo heels she owned—her calf-hugging, black leather, fuck-me boots with four-inch heels. The ones Kaylie had bought for her in an attempt to bring Danica over to the sexy side. She ran her finger over the stiletto heel and dropped her eyes to row after row of low-heeled, comfortable shoes. *Granny shoes. Hmph.* Maybe she had gone too far in the other direction, unsexing herself to distinguish herself from her clients. Danica pondered the thought as she went to lotion up her olive skin.

With her skin moisturized, her dress hiding her extra baggage, and a simple gold necklace, she surveyed herself in the mirror. Her boobs and hips looked in proportion. *God, this dress does work miracles.* Her hair was a mass of fuzz, with no way to tame it in sight. There was nothing she could do about that; she was born with hair like her father's, but on steroids. Her father's hair was coarse, like hers, with tight, little, perfectly formed curls. The kink and curls of her thick, dark hair were so different from her sister's and mother's straight, blond hair that she always felt a bit like an alien in her own family. But she couldn't go there now. Kaylie was waiting for her.

She grabbed her stiletto boots and reached for the light switch, eyeing the perfume and licorice on the bedside table. She hadn't had licorice for months, not since John. Boy was he ever a mistake. When they'd first begun dating, he'd been the perfect mix of a professional businessman and a spontaneous boyfriend. He'd taught Danica to loosen up, have fun, and even take a break from her nightly review of her clients' files. But four months into the relationship, he'd lost his job and seemed unable—or maybe unwilling—to stand on his own two feet. Danica found herself filling the role of therapist. Two months later, she'd finally extricated herself from the relationship and had quickly fallen back into her safe, careful ways. What had she been thinking? Licorice was her after-sex go-to food. She'd had a lot of licorice with John; at least the sex had been good, she mused. She threw the unopened bag of candy into her nightstand drawer and sprayed a quick spritz of Juicy Couture, a birthday gift from Kaylie when she was in her *we're-gonna-get-you-a-man* stage. That hadn't gone over very well. Danica had spent their evenings out looking over her shoulder for her clients instead of loosening up.

Now she wondered if she'd given herself a fair shot at a social life. One wrong man and her profession did not necessarily have to drive her to the lonely life of an old maid at twenty-nine. Before she knew it, she'd have a house full of cats and be one of *those* old ladies. The thought gave her pause. Maybe tonight she really would let herself have a little fun.

She inhaled, smiling with satisfaction at her image in the mirror, and headed for Bar None.

Kaylie grabbed Danica's hand as soon as she walked through the door and pulled her across the hardwood floor toward the bar, where the girls had gathered. It took all of Danica's attention to remain upright on her fuck-me heels. Maybe they were a mistake. When Kaylie finally stopped pulling her, she braced herself on the bar, preparing for the onslaught of hugs that would surely knock her off-kilter and send her sprawling onto the floor.

Dressed in a curve-hugging, dark blue dress with a neckline that plunged to her navel, Camille led the pack. She threw her arms around Danica. "You're here!" she squealed. Stephanie, Laurie, Chelsea, and Marie were right behind her with shrill shrieks and giggles. Danica swallowed her hatred of the fakeness that seemed to be an inherent part of most women. Their overly excited voices and dramatic waving of hands turned her stomach. Sometimes it made her feel like she was a lot older than her friends. *What is wrong with me?* Danica feigned the same artificial exuberance and hugged the friends she'd grown to love. A moment later she realized that she was excited to see them. Had she been repressing her enjoyment of the social aspects of life? *Okay, Danica. Turn off your therapist brain.* She was glad she had her stilettos on to level the playing field, because each of these girls was younger, hotter, and more confident than she was, especially in a bar.

Danica accepted a piña colada from Kaylie and took a gulp to calm her overactive nerves. Bars had never been within her comfort zone.

"We're drinking piña coladas and pretending we're in Aruba." She looked Danica up and down. "Where's the prim-and-proper Danica we all know and love? You look ravishing," Kaylie said as she slid onto a stool next to Danica.

"Like my nose?"

"What?" Kaylie laughed.

"This asshole elbowed me in the nose a few days ago, remember? I told you about it." Just like Kaylie to forget Danica's ten minutes of drama. "When I was going for coffee? I swear. Then, he had the gall to leer at some blonde as I stood there with blood all over my face."

"Really? What a jerk."

"No kidding." It felt good to unload her emotions on someone else for a change. Danica downed her drink and asked for another.

"Whoa, sis. Slow down. We have hours."

Danica looked at the other women. Camille, Stephanie, and Laurie were impossibly skinny, with collarbones poking out and not a speck of fat on their bare arms. Chelsea, Marie, and Kaylie looked like perfectly formed Barbie dolls—perky breasts, slim waists, and just the right amount of cushion in the trunk. Each were perfect for the handsome Blake. Danica put her arm over her stomach and reached for her drink.

Kaylie moved Danica's arm and whispered, "Stop it. You look great. You always worry about how you look, and you're stunning."

Danica rolled her eyes. "Right."

"You're a freakin' therapist and you can't even fix yourself. You've always been the exotic-looking one. I'm like plain Jane next to you." Kaylie touched a wayward curl on Danica's shoulder. "What I wouldn't do for your hair."

Danica took a drink. *If I had your body, the jerk wouldn't have looked at the blonde.*

Chapter Six

It was almost midnight when Blake finally hugged Sally one last time and told Rusty he'd take him to his basketball practices when he was ready to play again. He stepped out the front door of his dead best friend's house and into the frigid air. The door closed softly behind him. He pulled his shoulders up against the chill. A crushing guilt paralyzed him. He was alive and Dave wasn't. He stood there in the darkness, tears welling in his eyes, and sobs that he'd held in for the past several hours bubbling from his chest. He clenched his teeth against the sadness. He'd seen the woman Dave loved, seen the son he adored, hugged them, assured them he'd do anything he could to help them through the tragedy of Dave's death. And the whole time, all he could think about was how it should have been him that had died instead of Dave. It felt like a betrayal, being there with Dave's family. Blake had nobody waiting at home for him. He was just a blip on the radar screen of life, and once he was gone, he'd bet there wouldn't be many people who would cry for him. He was a selfish man, he realized. He'd been living his entire life caring only about himself and his own pleasures, never looking back at the hurt he caused others.

The woman he'd accidentally elbowed earlier in the week floated into his mind. The appalled look in her beautiful eyes when he'd glanced at the blonde came back to him. *Selfish*. He should have stopped Dave from going toward the back of the mountain. He should have considered that he might double back and take Little Hellion instead. If he'd been less self-absorbed, he might have pushed Dave to talk about the phone call, and then he might have realized that Dave's frustration would hinder his judgment.

The lights inside the modest two-story home went out. Blake stepped off the porch in a stupor of sorrow and guilt. His shoulders rounded forward as tears filled his eyes. He opened his car door and sat in the driver's seat, wanting desperately not to be alone.

Danica was on her third drink, feeling less inhibited and enjoying the feeling of having her guard down. She drank so rarely that she had an almost immediate reaction to it.

"Hey, there's Jeffrey and Mike." Kaylie pointed at Camille's fiancé. "Oh. My. God. Yummy, yummy." Kaylie stared beyond Jeffrey and Mike, to the entrance of the bar, where two men filed in like rowdy football players.

One of the men leaned down to hug a woman as he passed. Behind him, the man from the coffee shop came into clear view.

Oh shit.

"Dibs!" Kaylie squealed.

"Oh no, you do *not* want him. Trust me." Danica downed her drink, while Kaylie nursed hers.

"Are you kidding me? Want him? I *need* to taste him, feel him, own him—at least for a night or two." Kaylie's eyes danced with mischief. "Look at that body. Where on earth has he been hiding?" In a serious voice, she asked, "Do you know him? Can you introduce me?"

Danica's throat tightened. Behind Jeffrey and Mike, Blake was making a beeline for the bar, right where she and Kaylie were standing. She couldn't take her eyes off of him. This was impossible. Too coincidental.

"Danica, you look beautiful!" Jeffrey was the mirror image of Bradley Cooper. He was athletic, smart, witty, and very, very rich.

Danica kissed his cheek. "What are you doing here?"

"I can't let my fiancé go out alone on a Saturday night, can I? I brought my guys to make sure the bridesmaids weren't misbehaving." Behind him, his posse of groomsmen were greeting Kaylie and the others. Danica told herself that Adonis's presence was just a coincidence; he wasn't one of Jeffrey's groomsmen. They couldn't know each other, could they? Wouldn't she have known that? She'd seen the list of the bridal party and there was no Blake on it. Why, then, was he walking toward her, his eyes locked on hers, his goddamned gorgeous body coming closer by the second, rattling her nerves until her legs were trembling. She yanked at the hem of her dress, wishing she'd worn pants, something, anything to cover up her body a little more. Now that she was among the bold and the beautiful, she didn't feel quite as in proportion as she had in front of her mirror.

Kaylie elbowed her. "Here he comes!"

He was there, standing right in front of her in his black, button-down shirt and black slacks, his thick, wavy hair perfectly coiffed like Patrick Dempsey's. A smile spread across his cheeks; his teeth were like little, polished pearls, perfectly formed and as white as snow. *He knows he's hot. He's an egomaniac for sure.* But something was different from when she'd first seen him. His eyes had lost their roguish spark. He looked...sad. Surely she was misreading him. What did she know about him, anyway? This was probably his sullen pick-up look.

"Hi." Kaylie touched his forearm. "I'm Kaylie."

His green eyes flicked toward Kaylie, then right back to Danica. "Hi, Kaylie. I'm Blake."

"This is Danica," Kaylie said quickly.

Danica could actually feel her heart turning soft against her steeled reserve. His deep voice reeled her in. He leaned down and kissed Danica on the cheek. Tommy Hilfiger cologne assaulted her senses and weakened her knees.

"The nose looks better," he said.

"You're the one who bonked her nose?" Kaylie turned her back to Blake and mouthed to Danica, *That's the jerk?*

Danica nodded.

Kaylie mouthed, *Oh my God*, and her eyes sprang open wide.

"It's much better," Danica responded.

"I really don't make a habit of going around elbowing women. I'm sorry."

His swarthiness had toned down a notch. Her therapist senses came to attention. "It's okay. Are you with—" She pointed to Jeffrey, who was buying a round of drinks at the bar.

"Jeffrey? We know each other from college. He came by the shop the other day to get some gear and mentioned he'd be here tonight."

"Gear?" Danica asked.

Jeffrey handed a beer to Blake and piña coladas to Danica and Kaylie.

"Thanks, man," Blake said.

"I see you've met these lovely ladies," Jeffrey said. He turned toward Danica and answered, "Ski gear. Blake owns AcroSki, just down the block. I got to go give my girl a squeeze." He headed for the booth where the others had settled in.

Of course he does. Mr. Perfect, drop-dead gorgeous and a business owner.

"AcroSki? What's the Acro for?" Kaylie asked, as she slowly drank in every inch of Blake while she twirled her hair.

Danica watched Kaylie give Blake her best *I-wanna-fuck-you* look, her eyes soft and dark, the signature lick of her lips, and...*Don't do it. Don't entice a guy who I can't decide if I want to make out with or kick in the ass...Please don't do it.*

Kaylie dropped her finger from the end of her curl to her open neckline, then ran it along the crest of her breast and looked down, as if she'd had a tickle there.

Blake's eyes followed. "Acro, you know, for acrobatic?" He took a swig of his beer, shifting his eyes from Kaylie's breasts to Danica. He raised the beer bottle in her direction, as if to say, *Hey there.*

Danica's insides tightened. *Is he just being nice or flirting?* Kaylie would know the difference. Danica had no clue.

Kaylie touched his hand. "Wait. You actually do acrobatics on skis? Like jumps and stuff?"

Danica had seen that touch a thousand times. Next she'd laugh, throw her head back, and expose that gorgeous neck that men could not resist. Anger rose within her. Why was she angry? Let Kaylie have him. Who cared? She looked away in an effort to let go of the anger. Her eyes immediately found their way back to him. The simmering heat in her body remained.

"Jumps, flips, spins, you name it, I can do it." He shot a glance at Danica and winked.

"Of course you can," Danica snipped. *Asshole.* "He's all yours," she said to Kaylie, and didn't dare look at Blake for fear of finding yet another thing way too handsome to ignore. She felt his stare burning into her back as she headed for the nearby booth where Camille, Chelsea, Marie, and Stephanie were leaning head-to-head, drinks at the ready within their perfectly manicured fingers. They'd left their men behind for the girls' night out, and Danica wondered if they'd minded that Jeff had crashed their outing. Love drove Jeff there. She could see it in the glow in his eyes, and a nagging need in the back of her mind wanted to feel that same love.

She was proud of herself for walking away from Blake. The last thing she needed was a guy with roaming eyes...or anything else that tended to roam. A familiar feeling crept in like a giant spider, wrapping itself around her muscles and squeezing them so tightly that she wanted to scream. She bit back the jealousy she'd so often felt toward Kaylie and sat in the booth. While watching Kaylie and Blake out of the corner of her eye, she downed another drink and leaned in to hear what the girls were talking about.

"His name's Blake," Camille explained while the girls salivated.

Of course...

Chapter Seven

Blake watched Danica walk away and took another swig of his beer. She was feisty, with a killer body and the sexiest hair he'd ever seen. There weren't many women who walked away from him. In fact, he couldn't remember the last one who had. He watched her huddled with the other women at the table. He longed to touch her wild, unkempt hair, to slide his hand under that mass of curls and touch the hidden skin beneath. Why was he so drawn to someone who clearly did not like him?

"I would love to go with you sometime. Skiing, I mean. Maybe you could teach me how to do some of those tricks."

He turned back to Kaylie. The thought of hitting the slopes so soon after Dave's death turned his stomach. *Dave.* Blake closed his eyes for a minute, remembering Dave's anger as he'd stomped away. He couldn't believe he was really gone, and he didn't want to think about it now. It hurt too much. He snuck another glimpse at Danica. He needed something to keep his mind off of Dave's death, but Kaylie wasn't the answer. She was too sweet, too easy.

"I'm free this weekend. I mean, if you're going."

She was practically standing on top of him. Her straight, blond hair flowed like silk across her shoulders, a few manufactured curls spread throughout. He looked around the crowded bar and counted at least four guys staring at her. The competitive side of him reared up even though he wasn't sure he wanted her for himself. He gently touched her upper arm, staking claim, and at the same time, he glanced over at one of the men. The man immediately looked away. As he drew his eyes back to Kaylie, he skimmed the table where Danica sat nursing another drink.

Danica turned around. Their eyes locked. She squinted at him, not a friendly squint, more of a *how-dare-you* squint.

She turned away.

He realized he was still holding Kaylie's arm. He dropped his hand and said, "I'm not going skiing anytime soon." *I have to get out of here.*

"Well, we could still get together. I'm sure you have other tricks you could share with me," Kaylie said with a playful smirk.

Blake remembered his reflection in the mirror after the quickie with the redhead. He hadn't liked what he'd seen, and now, with the loss of his best friend, which he was desperately trying to forget for just a few more hours, the last thing he wanted was to be sexy and coy. He'd come to the bar on the prowl for an outlet, and Danica and this friend of hers were messing with his mojo.

He set his sights on Danica and chugged the rest of his beer, held it up toward the bartender, then sucked down half of the new one in one gulp. He felt caught between what would be the right thing to do—go home and mourn his friend—and the way his body was betraying him. He didn't want to be the guy who had meaningless sex with any beautiful and willing woman anymore, but his body was aching for the familiar release. With a woman in his arms, he could focus on the pleasure, maybe even turn his mind off completely, forget the pain of it all, and lose himself in the heat of the moment.

He eyed a blonde at the end of the bar. "Look, your friends are getting together. Why don't you join them?" He walked away, leaving Kaylie to stare after him, her jaw hanging open. He raised his beer in the direction of the blonde and she waved him over.

Danica steeled herself against the edge of the booth so Marie could get past her and go to the ladies' room. The floor swayed beneath her feet. Shit, she'd had a lot to drink.

Kaylie took the seat near where Danica stood and accepted a beer from the young, melon-boobed waitress. Kaylie's face was pinched tight. Danica tried to read her angry eyes but had a hard time focusing.

"Told you he was a jerk," she slurred.

"I'm fine, and he's not. He's just not interested." Kaylie sighed.

Blake sat at the bar with the blonde. His eyes darted over. Danica shot him a nasty sneer. "Only a douche wouldn't be interested in you." She swayed toward the booth.

Kaylie pulled her down to sit beside her. "Jesus, how many have you had?"

"I don't know. Three, four. Five, maybe? I'm fine. You always tell me to get out and live a little. That's what I'm doing. Living."

"I said you locked yourself up in your office too much. I never said to get sloshed and leave me to fend for myself." She looked in Blake's direction. "Can you believe he doesn't want me?" Kaylie pouted, pulling at the label on the beer bottle.

He wants anyone from nineteen to ninety-nine, guaranteed. Danica stared at the hunk of a man who was Blake Carter, trying to figure out why he rubbed her the wrong way—and why he also rubbed her in enough of the right ways to make butterflies swirl in her stomach like a lovesick teenager. The insanely big-boobed waitress handed him another beer. Blake leaned in close and said something in her ear. His fiery eyes shifted, then caught on Danica.

Just one look from his sexy, roving eyes was all it took. *Oh yeah, that's why.*

An hour later, Danica was dying to get home. She couldn't watch Blake, whom she'd renamed in her head as Mr. Arrogant, any longer. Two blondes flanked him at the bar. She looked around and wondered when Camille and the others had left. Had she been watching Blake the whole time? She remembered listening to bits and pieces of the conversations, and at some point someone handed her another drink. Heat ran up her chest. Was she *that* drunk?

Kaylie whispered in Danica's ear, "I'll call you tomorrow."

Danica peered around her little sister. In her drunken haze, the bar swirled. An adorable guy with dirty-blond hair was holding Kaylie's hand. "Who's that?" she slurred.

"Chaz. You okay to walk home?"

Danica swatted the air. "Sheesh, yeah, it's only a couple blocks. Go. Have fun." She watched Kaylie walk away and took that cue as her time to leave. She hadn't been this drunk since she and John broke up; it hadn't helped back then, either. She pushed to her feet as Blake and his entourage stood. He was heading her way, one arm around each of the women.

It's now or never. She pushed herself in the direction of the door, hoping to beat him to the exit.

"You okay to drive?" Blake asked as they came in step with her.

Damn heels. "I walked," she said, swaying on her feet.

"You sure you can make it?" He took a hand from around one skinny woman's waist and reached for Danica's arm to steady her.

Danica's heartbeat sped up. Goose bumps rushed up her arms, prickling her nerves and sending fire through her limbs. She looked into his smoldering eyes, his face inches from hers.

Each blonde had a hand on his back, placing claim.

"I'm good. Really. Thanks." *Let me go or I might kiss you. Where did that come from?*

Blake took his hand back, then said in a hushed, soothing voice, "Okay, but if you need me, I'm right here."

Oh yeah, I need you all right. Danica noticed that he didn't put his arms back around the women. She wanted to feel his hand on her again. She managed a nod, and he walked away between the two blondes, leaving her alone. *What else is new?*

Outside, she looked up and down the street. She'd been to Bar None a zillion times before, but tonight, too many piña coladas had stolen her sense of direction. She stumbled on her skyscraper heels and tumbled as she came off the curb, landing on her palms, her butt aiming up at the darkened sky.

"That's a great angle."

Blake. Danica pushed herself to her feet. Her ankle screamed out in pain, and she fell down to her butt on the side of the curb with an embarrassed gasp.

"Whoa." He sat down beside her, his leg touching hers.

She stared at his muscular thigh, feeling like a fool and wanting to touch him all at once.

"Those things are dangerous. Let me check your ankle." He moved off the curb and crouched in front of her. He lifted her leg at the knee and slid his hand over her ankle and up the sleek leather boot. She felt the heat of his palm all the way up the back of her calf. He slid them down slowly, as if he'd done it many times before, and slipped her stockinged foot carefully from the boot. Her foot dangled in the air between them.

Danica's head spun. It had been way too long since she'd felt her body react to a man's touch. She leaned back and closed her eyes. "It's fine," she whispered. One of his hands softly held her calf, sending a tingling sensation up her thighs. His other hand held her foot. His palms were warm and big. She wondered what they would feel like moving up her leg. Blake wiggled her foot, sending a searing pain through her ankle. Her eyes flew open. "Ouch!" She sat up and pulled her leg from his grasp, causing him to lose his balance and fall forward. He caught himself with his arms on either side of her waist, his face just above her chest. For a second, they just stared at each other. She held her breath, then realized he was doing the same.

He lowered his elbows, his lips coming closer to hers. "You okay?" he whispered.

His eyes bore into hers.

"You've asked me that a lot lately."

He smiled. "I guess I have."

God, he's impossibly gorgeous. Danica looked around, and even in her drunken state, she knew they must have been quite the sight splayed out along the curb of the side street in front of the bar. "We should move," she said, slipping off her other boot.

"Right." He pushed from the ground and then offered her a hand. Danica sat on the curb, unwilling to move. She didn't trust herself not to jump him. She felt like Belinda or Kaylie. All she could think about were his lips.

"Wait one second." He grabbed her boots from the ground. "Wow. No wonder you fell. These are killer heels."

"Where are your girlfriends?" she asked as she reached for his hand. The icy road beneath her bare feet made her shiver.

He pulled her to her feet, and she immediately collapsed back to the curb with a cry of pain.

"Uh-oh, you did do some damage. Want me to take you to the emergency room? It might be broken."

Emergency room? She couldn't think past the wonder of where his entourage was. She shook her head. "Where are your girlfriends?" she asked again.

"They're not my girlfriends. I can't help it if they clung to me." He sat down beside her, his shoulder touching Danica's.

She liked the feel of him. It had been so long since she'd been with a man. She'd almost forgotten the way a man's touch could make her heart soar. Maybe just this once, just one night? *Behave, woman*, she told herself. *Now you sound like Belinda. You know he's a player. Don't rationalize.*

"No emergency room. I'm fine. It's just twisted. I just need to get home. I live right around the corner, at The Heights condominiums. I can walk."

"No, you can't."

Pfft! She swatted the air. "I'm fine. Really, go."

"How about if I just drive you to your complex?"

Danica thought of Belinda again, and reality sobered her. "It's okay. I'll call a cab. Thanks, though."

"You sure? How about if I stay with you while you wait?" Blake looked at her with empathy, and Danica thought she saw desire hovering in his eyes.

"I'm really not that kind of girl, even if I'm drunk. Maybe you should have gone home with the Barbie twins."

Blake's jaw dropped. "Look, you don't even know me. I wasn't going to try anything, and I think that's pretty presumptuous of you." The hurt in his voice was palpable.

"I'm sorr—"

Blake was already heading for his car. He waved his hand dismissively behind him.

Great, now you can add *bitch* to your typically *frigid* self.

Chapter Eight

The morning light peeked in through the unfamiliar curtains. Blake slid off the bed and slithered into his jeans as silent as a mouse, a skill he'd spent the last twenty years refining. His head felt like a fog-filled balloon. He really needed to cut back on the tequila chasers. He tightened his belt around his slim waist and glanced in the mirror. He did a once-over, checking for fingernail marks, hickeys, or any of the other calling cards women left as their claim on him. No marks. A relieved sigh escaped his lips. He leaned over the dresser, closer to the mirror, and touched the peppery whiskers along his jaw. Yesterday he would have thought, *Damn. I've still got it.* Today, Blake saw an aging, selfish, lonely man. He'd spent the last several hours trying to escape the reality of his best friend's death, but now it found him like a vulture on prey, settling heavy and dark upon his shoulders.

He pulled his light-blue Henley over his thick, dark hair and smoothed it against the six-pack he worked so hard to maintain. With one last glance at the buxom brunette's shapely, bare ass, he headed for the door. He hadn't wanted to go home alone last night, and she'd been just what he needed. After that bitch Danica pegged him for just what he was, he'd needed a release and returned to the bar. *Get in, have fun, and get out*, he reminded himself. For all the years he could remember, that had been his motto. Dave had coined him as the Lady Slayer. Only, today, he wasn't on the high that he usually felt after a satisfying conquest. And Rozy, or Willow—he couldn't remember which—had definitely been satisfying. Today, he looked at her naked body and felt nothing but loneliness. Sally and Rusty would wake up soon and realize that Dave was really gone. Blake knew he couldn't run from the hurt that was clawing at his heart, but he could ignore it.

Blake pulled away from her apartment in his Land Rover, thinking about Dave. The sadness hit him like a punch to the gut. He'd hoped to run from the hole Dave had left in his life and from the pain of thinking about it, but he'd woken up as the exact same man he'd been the night before, only, if possible, even lonelier. He had to go to work and face a business that would only emphasize the loss of his friend. He wished he could go from one bed to the next, occupying his mind on the plays he put on women, pretending as if the real world didn't exist. But even he knew that one day that hurt would find him, and he'd drown in an even deeper abyss of mourning chased by a helping of self-loathing.

Blake stood in front of the glass doors of AcroSki, his feet rooted to the ground. Once he walked inside, he knew real life would find him. He wasn't ready to deal with it. He'd pushed his feelings down to a manageable flicker, and he knew that the moment he opened those doors and was welcomed by darkness and silence, that flicker would burst into flames and burn right through his coat of armor.

The sign on the door said Closed, as it had since they'd closed up and headed for the slopes the night of Dave's accident. The moments before they'd skied came rushing back to him—Dave's anger, Blake's dismissal of that anger. *Dave would never walk through those doors again.* Blake was surprised at how his heart slammed within his chest, and his hands began to tremble. He could not do it. He couldn't face customers and pretend everything was okay. He'd tried to pretend last night and this morning, but it was right in front of him again. He had to take the day off. He couldn't work. He mentally ticked off what he'd have to accomplish in order to make that happen. He'd lose income, but that wasn't a problem. He had plenty of money. He'd have to pay their two part-time employees. It was only fair. Within minutes, he'd made his decision. He would escape reality for one more day, but there was something inside that he needed, and that meant entering into the silence.

Blake tightened the muscles in his legs, pulled his shoulders back, and turned the lock. *I can do this.* He walked through the doors into the cool air of the store. The temperature was always cooler in the mornings, before the timer for the heat kicked up a notch. With his head down, he barreled toward the office, trying to ignore the absence of Dave's banter: *Hey, Lady Slayer. Who was it last night? Brunette or blonde?* Blake went into the office, flicked on the light, and closed the door, leaving the ghost of his best friend behind him. His chest rose and fell with each heavy breath. He pushed around the papers on his desk, frantically pulled the drawers open one by one, then sifted through the documents inside. *Where the hell is it?*

He thought about the day before, the slip of paper Dave shoved into his pocket. What had he done with it? *Damn it!* He had to find it fast. He wanted to make an appointment with someone to help him modify his behavior before he changed his mind. He needed to lock himself in this time with more than just words.

Blake picked up the phone and called their employees, breaking the news of Dave's death. They needed their own time to mourn, so closing the store had come as no surprise to them. He jogged back through the store, then out the front doors, locking them—and Dave's missing presence—behind him. The Closed sign swayed against the glass. He knew he'd have disappointed customers, but he was dead set on dealing with this head on. Adrenaline sent him running for his car. He climbed in, breathing hard. He was doing the right thing. He knew he was. Dave's death was the impetus he needed to make some changes in his life. He pushed the pedal to the floor and was home in twenty-eight minutes.

He flew up the stairs to his third-floor condo and unlocked the door. He breezed through and didn't even notice when the door slammed shut behind him. He ran to his laundry basket, throwing dirty clothes onto the floor until he found his jeans, then dug into each pocket until the slip of paper came out in his fingers. He let out a loud breath and closed his fist around it.

Blake sat on the chocolate-brown comforter on his king-sized bed and leaned his elbows on his knees, his forehead pressed into his fisted hands. He contemplated his next move. Did he really need help? Couldn't he just deal with Dave's death like other people did? Let the ache and the missing come in and spirit him away into a deep depression? He would go about his life as he always had—from one woman to the next, ignoring his emotions. Feeling nothing but a cocoon of his own pleasure. What was so wrong with that?

He opened his fist and looked at the crumpled paper. Dave's meticulous handwriting stared back at him, his voice floating forth. *Work through that mommy drama of yours.* Blake hadn't thought of his mother, really thought of her, in years. She'd left when he was just a little boy. He lay back on the bed and closed his eyes. Dave was gone. Really gone. He'd been his only real friend.

Everyone else was transient, peripheral, benign. A tear slipped down his cheek. He swiped at it angrily. Damn it. He wasn't a child. People died! It was just part of life. He stood and paced.

His cell phone rang. He glanced at it. *Sally. Shit.* He let it go to voice mail, then dialed the number on the slip of paper. He needed to be strong for Sally, and in his current state of mind, he just couldn't be. His heart pounded against his chest. One ring. Two. He could hang up now. Three. *Just hang up.* Voice mail. *You've reached the office of Dr. Snow...*

"Hi, um...I'd like to make an appointment, please." He added his phone number and took the phone away from his ear, then brought it back. "Thank you." He pressed End, then realized he hadn't left his name. There was no way he was calling back. He didn't trust himself not to cancel the inquiry.

He dialed Sally's number.

Chapter Nine

Danica and Michelle sat by the window in Crumbles Bakery, surrounded by the homey aroma of coffee and freshly baked bread. Because Michelle's past was so traumatic, Danica tried to find cozy places for them to meet. She believed that smells and surroundings could have an impact on one's mood, though if Michelle's mood was any indication, she'd been dead wrong. Danica enjoyed being Michelle's Big Sister. It was a different experience from being Kaylie's older, biological sister. She looked at Michelle, slumped over the table, with her straight, bottle-black hair hanging down to the middle of her back. Their thirteen-year age difference made her more like an aunt than a sister, but Danica was still younger than Michelle's mom, which made her more relatable. That might be why they got along so well. Sometimes, they just sat and talked for hours, and other times they went to the movies, bookstores, or museums.

She thought again about the youth center she had longed to open and wondered, if there were such a place, would Michelle feel like she fit in?

Michelle broke off pieces of the apple-cinnamon muffin before her, dropping the fingertip-sized pieces onto her tongue.

"So, what's new? How's Nola?" Michelle had lived with her grandmother Nola since her mother had gone into the rehab facility. Danica tried to ignore her pounding hangover.

Michelle shrugged, her eyes still trained on the muffin.

"Is her health okay?"

Michelle pursed her lips and nodded.

It usually took a few minutes for Michelle to open up each week, but today she appeared more sullen than usual. She wore her signature black jeans and baggy, black T-shirt.

"So, what else is new with you? Is school okay?" Danica pushed.

Michelle looked up at Danica quickly, then back down at the table.

Bingo! "Anything you want to talk about?" Danica asked.

Michelle shook her head.

They sat in uncomfortable silence for several minutes, until Michelle lifted her eyes, staring up at Danica from behind her thick, dark bangs.

"School sucks." She dropped her eyes.

Success! "Yeah, it does suck. I remember high school. Everyone wants to be invisible, and those who don't are so obnoxious that you wish you could just tell them off—which, of course, would be social suicide."

Michelle smiled.

Danica knew she was finally getting through. She gained a different type of satisfaction when dealing with Michelle than when she dealt with her paying clients. It was so difficult to be a teenager, with what could feel like insurmountable peer pressures and hormones driving them in new and different directions. Sometimes she rued her decision to follow her parents' guidance and take the financially safe route of being a therapist. But that was water under the bridge, so she'd focus on helping Michelle as best as she could. "I remember wanting to wear the right clothes, say the right thing, date the right guys."

Michelle's smile faded.

"But I never could—date the right guys, I mean. The ones who were popular were assholes, and I wasn't really attracted to the ones who weren't. Gosh, that sounds bad. It's not like I had many choices. I was even nerdier then than I am now." Danica took a sip of her coffee. "If that was even possible." She thought of those painful years, remembering how Kaylie sailed through high school in a sea of happiness, with too many friends to count.

"You probably had tons of boyfriends," Michelle said.

"Nope. They called me Danica Manica because I was flat as a board with no hips and awful hair."

Michelle sat back in her seat. "You're so pretty. I can't imagine that."

Danica shook her head. "Thank you, but believe me, I was queen nerd and wasn't at the top of anyone's dating list."

They both laughed.

"What about you? You must have guys who are interested?" Danica wished she could brush Michelle's hair out of her sad, hazel eyes.

Michelle shook her head. "I'm a pariah. I'm known as *that girl whose mother is an alchie.*"

Hurt pierced Danica's heart. No kid should have to go through that. "They can't blame you for your mother's illness."

"Illness?"

"Well, yeah, alcoholism is like a disease. Your mom can't really help it. She's struggling with addiction. But I guess that's a bit much for high school kids to understand. Your mom's out of rehab, so at least you know she *wants* to stop drinking." This was the second time Michelle's mother had been in rehab, which didn't necessarily equate to a permanent pattern. Danica didn't have all of the details of Nancy's recent stint in rehab, but she did know that Nancy had signed herself in. She hadn't been forced to go. A permanent change was never easy, but Danica was hopeful.

"How can I not blame her? It was her choice to drink in the first place." Michelle tapped her foot.

Danica watched Michelle scanning the bakery for an escape. The last thing she wanted was for her to feel trapped. "Let's get out of here."

They walked side by side down the busy sidewalk, and Danica found herself scanning the passersby for Blake. Then she chided herself for doing so. Sometimes Danica wished they didn't live in a tourist trap, where people meandered rather than walked with a purpose. That was one of the main reasons she usually stuck to non-touristy spots. The other reason was that she worked so much that she rarely had time to spend at trendier locations.

She looked at their reflections in the windows of the restaurants and shops as they passed. Michelle walked with her shoulders hunched, hands shoved deep into her pockets. Danica looked like she'd come directly from work, in her thick, wool blazer and slacks. She looked like she could almost be Michelle's mother. She cringed at the thought of looking any older than she already was.

"What do you want to do today? I thought we might do a little shopping." Danica hoped to eventually get Michelle out of the ninja clothes she hid behind.

Michelle crinkled her nose.

"A movie?"

"Um, do you think we could go to that museum again?" Michelle asked tentatively.

"Sparks? You liked that?" Danica had taken her to the little eclectic art museum months ago. Michelle hadn't seemed too interested then, and Danica was surprised she'd want to return. They turned the corner and headed for the museum.

Danica held the door to Sparks open for a couple to leave and for Michelle to enter. The pungent aroma of patchouli filled the small lobby. Michelle walked straight through the lobby and toward the back of the museum. Danica fell in step behind her as they passed enormous iron and clay sculptures in the main hall and filed through an adjoining narrow hallway lined with paintings and smaller sculptures set on tall, black, rectangular bases. She wondered if Blake liked art. She envisioned him in a thick ski parka, running his hand through his hair and feeling right at home surrounded by the smell of patchouli. *Generalizations, much?* She had to get him out of her mind.

Off of the hallway were several small exhibit rooms, no larger than a typical bedroom, lined floor to ceiling with various types of artwork. That was part of the aura of Sparks that she loved. Entering Sparks was like entering another world, like convention had yet to be conceived.

Michelle stopped in front of an abstract painting. She stood with her hands in her oversized, black-canvas coat pockets, her head cocked at an angle.

Danica mimicked her stance, trying to make sense of the art. She had trouble understanding abstract things that weren't part of a person's being or emotions, but she knew that art was a great way to express feelings, and she'd been right to hope Michelle might enjoy it. Kaylie had gotten the artistic genes in the family. That's why Danica loved working with people who could relay what they were thinking—even if they didn't realize that what they said wasn't exactly what troubled them. People were easy for Danica. She could tell when someone was twisted in knots and needed help finding the way to straighten their spine. Art, not so much.

"What do you think it represents?" Danica asked.

Michelle shrugged. "I just like looking at it."

Danica was glad that Michelle was taking interest in something. Now, if she could only get her talking. "Does it remind you of anything?" She looked at the picture, turning her head one way, then the other. There were two eyes, but they were floating amidst what looked like a child's painting of fish gone wrong and uneven streaks, with splotches of colors and what looked like two mouths eking out of the corners of the canvas. Something that looked strangely like a three-fingered hand reached down from the top edge.

Michelle glanced over with a wrinkled brow. "I'm not sure. I just remember it from last time, and I like it."

Danica walked around the little room, secretly watching Michelle. Michelle crossed her arms, then uncrossed them. She put her hands on her hips, then dropped them, as if her arms were some sort of strange appendages that she wasn't used to. She obviously felt out of place in school, hadn't had a boyfriend the entire time Danica had known her, and wasn't about to open up today. Come to think of it, Danica hadn't had a boyfriend in an even longer time. *No time for one*, she reminded herself, and thought about the files she'd review later in the afternoon. Her professional life had seeped into every spare moment she had. Maybe it was time for a change, she mused.

Danica had to find a way to break through to Michelle. She sidled up next to her. "Maybe it reminds you of your life? You know, all the pieces are there, but you can't really make sense of them right now?"

"Whatever," Michelle said, and walked out of the room with Danica on her heels.

Danica's cell phone buzzed, indicating a new message had been left on her office voicemail. She'd be sure to check it as soon as she was done spending time with Michelle.

Two hours later, Danica and Michelle stood on Nola's front porch. Michelle opened the door, and a familiar smell that Danica likened to the smell of old people's houses—a mixture of mothballs, too-warm air, and floral perfume—wafted out the door of the small brick rambler. Danica made a mental note to remember that Michelle was only fourteen and the smell of patchouli was probably cool and fun to her while Grandma's house was the epitome of someplace she wouldn't want to bring friends to visit. She'd have to find someplace hip to take her next week. Maybe she'd ask Kaylie for a suggestion.

Chapter Ten

At seven o'clock Monday morning, Danica sat in her office reviewing the file of her first client and ignoring the flashing red message light on her phone. She always arrived early to prepare for the day, and most days she had a client come in before they had to go to their own job. She set the file down on her neatly organized desk and glanced at the time. Like every morning, she had just enough time to run down to the local café and grab a cup of coffee before her client arrived. She stared at the blinking light. She'd already let it go overnight. Ever since Saturday night, Danica had been thinking about trying to strike a balance between work and some sort of social life. Who was she kidding? She had no social life, and the one time she tried to go out and pretend to have one, she'd obviously gone way overboard and drank too much, which she not only regretted, but was terribly embarrassed about. Not answering her messages over the weekend was one of the changes she hoped to make. Reclaiming her weekends was a good start, she decided, but as she noticed the time—7:07—her foot tapped and her heart raced. It was one thing to leave messages until after the weekend, but it was officially Monday morning, and early or not, she was in work mode. She bit her lower lip, fighting the urge to retrieve the message.

It was Monday. Someone needed something. She grabbed the phone, pushed the blinking light, and retrieved the message from a new client. She scribbled down the phone number and dialed the phone.

"Hello?" a deep voice answered.

"Hi, this is Dr. Snow. Uh, um..." She realized that there was no name left on the machine and hesitated to say much more in case the person who called needed discretion. Thankfully, she didn't have to fill the gap.

"Oh. Thanks for calling back. I wanted to make an appointment."

He sounded tired. *Didn't they all?* "Sure. Can you please tell me what you're hoping to get help with?"

"I...uh...my best friend just died. I think I need to talk about it."

She listened to him breathe and knew that he needed her to take charge. "I'm sorry for your loss." She flipped through her calendar. She had time today at two o'clock, but she'd hoped to get out and buy Michelle a black shirt that wasn't so...grungy looking. "I can see you tomorrow at three or Friday at one thirty."

"Oh." Disappointment sifted through the airwaves. "I was hoping to start sooner."

"Are you having suicidal thoughts?" Her ears perked up. Even after all her years of experience, she couldn't find a more tactful way to ask the most important questions.

"What? No." He sighed. "To be honest, I'm afraid I might back out of the appointment if I think about it too much. But I know I need it."

That made sense. She'd had too many cancellations to count, and she'd worried about each one of them for days afterward. That was another thing she had to work on, letting go of the people who didn't want her help. "Okay." She sighed. "Today at two is the only time I have this afternoon. You should be aware that I don't take insurance. My address is—"

"I know just where you are. Thank you. I'll be there." He hung up the phone.

Danica stared at the receiver. She hadn't even gotten his name. She set the receiver down and scribbled *new client* in her appointment calendar, adding *friend died,* and then wrote down the phone number next to the note.

Chapter Eleven

Blake stood in front of Dr. Snow's office door. He lifted his hand to knock, then realized he had no idea of the proper etiquette at a therapist's office. What if right inside the door was her desk and a couch that he'd need to sit down on. *Sit down?* What if people really did lie down on the couch? What was typical? Normal? His chest constricted with discomfort.

He looked at the stairs behind him and thought about fleeing. She had his phone number. He could leave a message and say he was ill, or stand her up and miss the appointment. *Juvenile.* Sally had called earlier, and his heart had nearly broken through his chest, he'd been so nervous. He'd rushed off the phone, claiming he was busy, but the truth was that he didn't even know how to act with her. Cheerful? Sad? Consolatory? He was an emotional idiot.

Blake knew that the first year after AcroSki's opening had been difficult for Sally. Their income hadn't taken off until after they'd paid back the bank loan they'd taken to buy the store, but Sally had never complained. She'd supported Dave, even with the late evenings it took to get the store off the ground. She'd bring dinners for them when they worked late, and she'd always included Blake. He needed to do this. For Dave. For Sally. For himself.

Just as Blake reached for the knob, the door swung open. A short, wide-eyed, heavy man—looking as startled as Blake felt—stood before him. The man dropped his gaze to the floor.

"She's all yours," the man said, as he hurried past Blake.

Blake walked into the small reception area. Four chairs, two on each side of the room, separated by an antique coffee table, gave the room a homey feel. He stepped inside and closed the door quietly behind him. Blake looked over a wooden bookshelf filled with self-help books that sat against the far wall, wondering if he'd made a mistake. He sat down in one of the chairs. The room was eerily silent, save for a white noise machine. He crossed his ankle over the opposite knee, then dropped it to the floor. He checked his watch: 1:55. There was a door on the wall opposite the entrance. He stared at it. *Dr. Snow is back there*. What if she was really hot? Could he tell her about himself? What if she was hideously ugly? Would that make it easier? Or more difficult because she might feel bad about her own looks?

He looked back at the entrance door. Every fiber of his being willed him to rise and go out that door. *Just go. Leave. This isn't for you.*

Danica set a fresh notepad and pen on the edge of her desk, then went to the door, smoothing her black pencil skirt and colorful blouse. She opened the door and walked out smiling, her typical welcome to new clients rolling off her lips.

"Hi, I'm Dr. Snow." Her smile faded. Her heart pounded. It was *him.*

Blake laughed. "Well, this is awkward."

Danica didn't know what to say. She'd never had this issue before. Should she tell him she couldn't help him? *Why?* he'd ask. She'd answer, *Because I think you're really hot. Because all I've thought about for the past twelve hours are your lips.* Shit. She could do this. There was nothing between them. He needed help, and that was her job. *Grow up.*

"Nah, awkward? Come on in. We'll talk." She led him into the office, then realized she needed to give him an out, just in case he was feeling as uncomfortable as she was.

Blake sat in one of the leather chairs opposite the desk. Danica sat in the chair across from him. She never sat behind the desk when meeting with clients, she found it too much of a barrier. Though now, she wished she'd sat behind the desk. A barrier might be nice.

"Okay, so, I'm a therapist. Surprise." She forced a smile. "You're here for help, but given the recent," she elbowed the air, "and," she lifted her ankle, "if you're uncomfortable, I can refer you to someone else if you'd like." *Please don't go. Go. No, don't.* She didn't realize she was holding her breath until he answered.

"Actually, I think this might be good for me." He crossed his arms over his chest.

Reflectively, Danica noted his posture and had to keep from jumping into the same protective position. She caught herself looking at his arms and reached for the pad and pen on the edge of her desk.

"How does this work?" Blake asked.

This, she could handle. "Well, I usually start with my intake paperwork. Typical questions. And you'll need to fill out this information." She handed him a clipboard with the necessary disclosures. "Why don't you fill that out first, and then we can talk." She moved to sit behind her desk, needing the barrier more than she'd thought.

"Okay. Here? Or do you want me to fill this out in the waiting room?" He stood.

"Wherever you want. They literally take just a few minutes."

For a moment neither one moved. The air between them was thick—not uncomfortable, not electrified— just as if a bubble had formed between them and neither one quite knew how to maneuver around it.

"Okay, then." Blake sat back down.

Danica turned her back to him and pretended to look through the files on her credenza. *You can do this. Calm down. Think, client. Client. Client.*

"Okay, that was easy." He set the clipboard on the desk, and Danica came back around and sat down. She flipped through the paperwork. *Thirty-four, single, no meds, ski shop owner, no history of anything unusual.* Danica cleared her throat, thinking, *Except being a player, maybe.*

She took a deep breath and blew it out slowly. "Thanks. Blake, what are you here for? You said your friend died?" She found herself slipping into her therapist persona easier than she'd thought possible.

Blake looked down at his hands, then back up at her. *God, he's handsome. Stop it!*

"Yes, Dave, my friend." He paused and looked around her office. "Dave Tuft was my best friend. He died in a skiing accident on Saturday."

"Saturday?" She couldn't keep the surprise from her voice. "But you were at the bar last Saturday night. I saw you, remember?"

"Avoidance," Blake said with a straight face. "It's one of my...one of the things I need to work on. Look," Blake leaned forward, his elbows on his knees, "I'm not someone who doesn't see his own faults. I know I'm a...I've been a bit of a..."

Danica raised an eyebrow, secretly reassessing what she thought of him by his honesty. She had little tolerance for lies, although in this case, lies might make her job much easier. She'd instantly be turned off by lies, while honesty was harder to resist.

"Well, I'm *that* guy."

Come on. You can do it, Blake. "That guy?" Danica was not going to spoon-feed any client, including him. Especially him. She couldn't wait to hear if he fessed up to being the person she saw him as.

"*That* guy. You know. The one who dates a different girl every night. The one who accidentally hits a woman in the nose, then looks at another woman while she's standing there bleeding."

So, he did know what he was like. "Before we talk about all of that—and we will talk about all of that—I'd like to get an idea of your familial background."

Blake groaned and leaned back in his chair.

"I'm not a therapist who believes that you need to relive your childhood in order to make progress, but I do like to know what you've experienced, so I can better help you." She pulled off her normal speech without a hitch. *That was easy.* Danica squeezed her pen so tight that her knuckles stung. This was where the bad guys came out. Molestation, emotional abuse, any of the triggers from childhood could bring even the strongest man to tears—or to aggression. She watched for the telltale signs of the latter while he answered.

"I know I have to talk about this, but it's difficult." He took a deep breath, and Danica watched a brief look of pain pass through his eyes. "My mom left when I was three."

"Have you seen her since?"

Blake shook his head. "She didn't leave a forwarding address. I lived with my father." Blake looked out the window, his eyes serious, as if he was contemplating something. When he turned back toward Danica, she saw the same softness she'd caught a glimpse of when he'd first elbowed her in the café. "He did the best he could. Worked two jobs, spent time with me. I'm not a kid who was ignored or abused."

That helps. She waited patiently for him to continue. All clients had this lull in admission. Danica knew better than to prompt them. How they continued was often very telling.

"I don't see him much. He moved away, and I—"

Danica waited, listening to the faint road noise filtering in through the closed windows. She waited until his discomfort with the silence became evident in his fidgeting. She was used to this. Blake fidgeted. She waited.

"Hell, I don't know. There's no real reason we don't see each other except probably that he's old and I'm selfish."

Yes! One point for being self-aware! She nodded, hiding her enthusiasm for his honesty and wondering what he might be hiding. Everybody was hiding something. "Okay, so no mom growing up, and Dad was a good guy. That's all I need for now to be able to move forward." She set the clipboard down on her desk and relaxed a bit, steepling her hands beneath her chin. "Tell me about Dave."

Blake's eyes went from serious to sad, then settled on something in between. "He was my business partner. We skied together."

Danica nodded, waited.

He looked down, then spoke softly. "He would egg me on, with women, you know? But then, in the same breath, he'd hint that I shouldn't be doing what I was doing." Blake locked eyes on Danica. "He's the reason I'm here. He gave me your number before he...before the accident."

"Well, he sounds like a good guy. I'm sorry that you lost him. That must be very painful. Do you want to talk about the accident?" Danica felt herself warming to him, like she had to Keith Small, a previous client. An alcoholic who went to every AA meeting with the hope of actually changing, even though he still went home and drank. It had taken over a year of working with him, but he'd eventually gone through rehab and was now living a sober lifestyle. She saw the same hope in Blake's eyes. She's seen that look many times before. While tragedy was a major catalyst, few clients actually remained steadfast in their path to change after the initial shock of losing someone wore off.

Blake shook his head. "Not really."

She could barely take her eyes off of him. *How could one man be so attractive?* "Okay, Blake, what would you like to share with me?" *My bed? Jesus Christ, where did that come from? This is not a good idea.*

"My other...habits." He leaned back again, crossing his arms. "This is weird, isn't it? Talking about this stuff after you've seen me with those women? I mean, if this is awkward for you, we don't have to talk about this."

"Blake, this is my job. I see you as a client, and I'm happy to help you with these issues. But as I said when you came in, if you are uncomfortable, please, by all means, let me refer you to someone else." Danica should have felt relieved; instead she felt competitive. She was damn good at her job, and she vowed to treat him like any other client. No more dirty thoughts. Danica didn't see him as a client yet, but she'd push past her sinful stirrings and remain on the professional side of that ominous, thin, gray line that every therapist had to respect. She could be his therapist. She was the best therapist in town, at least she liked to think so.

Blake looked at her, nodding, considering. He leaned forward, then back again. "You're sure?"

"Yes, I'm sure. Listen, I've helped—for lack of a better word—*players* before. While that might be something you want to work on, I feel like there's more here than just what you do in your spare time. You've lost your friend, someone who obviously meant a lot to you. Maybe that's where we should start, when you're ready."

"Maybe. But I'm not ready."

"Okay. Do you want to continue today's session? We have another fifteen minutes. Or we could end today's here and you can take some time to figure out if you wish to continue with me."

Blake stood, and Danica fought the urge to reel off her credentials: PhD in clinical psychology from Boston University, undergrad degree from Tufts.

He shook Danica's hand with a firm grip. Danica stood tall, her shoulders back, queen of her therapist domain. "I'm glad you came in." Then she added, just to solidify the professional relationship, "I'll drop your bill in the mail."

Blake nodded. "Thank you," he said, and headed for the office door. He stopped before opening it and said, "It was nice to see you again." He smiled, and Danica felt her professional posture slipping away. She cleared her throat to settle her nerves.

"Yes, you too. And I'm sorry about your friend." Danica watched him walk out the door, and when it was firmly closed, she collapsed into her chair, letting out a long, relieved sigh. *Blake Carter.* Her nerves tickled with delight. He was right there, in her office. Is this what all the fuss was about with Kaylie and Belinda? That heat that began in your thighs and traveled up to your chest, feeling like it might explode? Now she understood. She stood and paced, her arms crossed, a smile painted across her cheeks. Her cell phone rang, reeling her excitement in like a fishing line.

She picked up the phone. *Kaylie.* "You won't believe who was just in my office," she gushed.

"Arnold Schwarzenegger? Kate Middleton? Dane Cook?" Kaylie laughed.

"Blake Carter."

"What? Why?" Kaylie asked, suddenly drained of her enthusiasm.

That's when it hit Danica like a brick in the face. She either had to get ahold of herself or drop him as a client—if he even ever came back. "I can't tell you. I shouldn't have even said anything. Damn it." What had she been thinking? It would be a challenge, but she was up to it. She was not the kind of therapist to lose her license over a blip of bad judgment.

"What the hell, sis? I tell you everything."

Danica heard Kaylie's hurt through the telephone line. "No, I mean, I can't reveal why he came, just that he was here."

"Oh my God, really? Are you going to see him as a client? Isn't that wrong or something?" Kaylie's voice turned serious.

"Not necessarily. His friend referred him, and we have no prior relationship. He hit me in the nose and we talked at the bar. That's as far as it went."

"Come on. Isn't that like saying you only sort of had sex? Who are you now, Bill Clinton?"

Danica didn't like the insinuation, even if she was a little bit right. Had they kissed, Danica would not have taken him on as a client, but there'd been no physical contact. Hell, she didn't even know if she liked him, except for his looks. Maybe that wasn't exactly true, but she was a professional. She could determine whom she'd fall into bed with and whom she wouldn't, and Blake was now officially off limits.

"No, it's not the same thing at all. Look, the guy needs help, and maybe I'll help him. I'm not even sure if I'm going to take him on as a client or not."

"What if he likes you and he's only making up whatever he's there for to get closer to you?"

Kaylie had a wild imagination. Danica mulled over the idea for a second, instantly rejecting it as ridiculous. "He didn't even know it was me he was calling. It's fine. Really."

"If you say so."

"Anyway, what are you calling for?" she asked.

"Oh, I almost forgot. Chaz is going with me to the Indie Rock Fest next weekend. Wanna go?"

Kaylie was always jetting off somewhere. "In Atlanta? Who's Chaz?"

"Uh-huh, and you know Chaz. The guy I met at Bar None."

"Right. Kaylie, you've known this guy what—a day and a half? You don't know anything about him. Is that even safe?"

"Come on, *Mom*. I'm twenty-seven years old. I think I can make that judgment call. I just don't get you. Why can't you break out and have a little fun? Just because Mom and Dad always said you were the smart, responsible one doesn't mean that's who you have to be."

Did it mean that's who she had to be? Danica wondered. Had she lived up to their desires rather than being who she wanted to be? Was she living a self-fulfilled prophecy? Was everyone? She thought of her hopes for the youth center. Danica shook the thoughts from her head, unable to filter through them in her present state of mind. She needed to focus on what mattered, and she had a client coming in shortly. "I did that, remember? Saturday night? What did that get me? A freakin' hangover the size of Washington, DC."

"So what? It was fun, wasn't it?" Kaylie mocked. "Just get over yourself and come with me, already."

Danica pictured Kaylie's smug expression, her eyes saying, *Come play with me*, her body language daring her with her arms crossed and lips pursed, pushing Danica to be just like her and shirk her responsibilities. Then again, Kaylie had hardly any responsibilities when compared to Danica. Kaylie's whole life was spontaneous. "Well, as much as I'd like to be your chaperone—and trust me, I would—I can't. I take Michelle out on Sundays, remember? Which reminds me, where can I take a teenager that would be really fun?"

"Indie Rock Fest," Kaylie said with a serious tone.

"You're no help. I gotta get ready for my next client. Call ya later?"

"She'd have a great time," Kaylie urged.

"Gotta go. Love you."

Chapter Twelve

Two nights later, Blake sat at Sally's kitchen table, fidgeting with his keys, a full cup of coffee in front of him. Sally had aged ten years in the few days since Dave's death. She sat with her hands wrapped around a steaming mug, a thick, white cardigan pulled tight across her thin body. She reached up and brushed a strand of her white- blond hair from her forehead. She wore no makeup. On anyone else, her pale skin might have looked weak or worn-out. But even in her state of loss, Sally looked regal. Blake remembered all of the times he'd jokingly called her Dave's trophy wife, and now he felt bad for making fun.

"Thanks for taking Rusty to basketball. He fought me on it. He doesn't want to go, but I think it's important to go on with our lives as best we can. I don't want Rusty to lose his friends because of his father's death. It's too easy to fall into depression at his age." She looked up with sad, robin's-egg blue eyes. "He's already got all that teenage angst going on."

"It's not a problem. I have nothing better to do," Blake said, and at this point, he really didn't have anything better to do. He'd promised himself he would refrain from his womanizing. "If you're sure he's ready."

Sally nodded. "To some degree, Rusty needs this outlet. He and Dave had an argument right before...the accident."

Blake remembered the bits and pieces of Dave's last phone call on the slopes. He'd assumed all parents dealt with the ups and downs of hormone-filled teenagers, but that being the last conversation Rusty had with his father was too much for anyone, much less a teen to shoulder. "Then I'm happy to do it."

Sally stood and put her mug in the sink, her back to Blake. She wrapped her arms around her body, and Blake watched her shoulders go up and down with a deep inhalation. When she turned around, her eyes were serious, her lips set in a straight line. "Blake," she said, then squinted, as if thinking about what she was about to say.

"Yeah?"

Rusty came into the kitchen wearing sweatpants and a black, hooded sweatshirt. His blond hair, just a shade darker than Sally's, was long and straight, the way guys wore their hair in the seventies. His face was drawn and tired. "Ready?"

Sally shook her head in Blake's direction. "Nothing." She went to Rusty, standing eye to eye to with her son. "Try and have fun, okay? Blake's ready, and I'll be here when you get home."

Rusty turned away.

"I love you, Russ." Sally's voice was almost a plea rather than a statement. She wrapped her arms around her middle as Blake stood to leave with Rusty. "Thanks, Blake. Call me if you need me."

Blake didn't know much about teens, and he was certain his experience of losing a parent was probably different from Rusty's. Sally adored him, and Dave had created a world that seemed to revolve around him, while Blake had a mother who'd abandoned him and a father who was always working. Blake couldn't imagine that his mother's abandonment was too similar to Dave's death. He was afraid to assume that it might fuel the same type of resentment, but he had to say something. Once again, Blake wished he were more adept at handling the things in life that required emotions.

"I'm real sorry about your dad, Rusty," Blake said as they drove toward the high school.

Rusty stared out the passenger window, his hands stuffed in his sweatshirt pockets. He didn't respond.

Okay, dad is off-limits. "So, what position do you play?" he asked.

Rusty turned toward him. His square jaw looked identical to Dave's, but he'd clenched it so tight that it looked out of place on his youthful face. Sally's blue eyes looked back at him—pained and unmistakably angry. "Center." He turned back toward the window.

Blake nodded, wanting to lighten the mood. He couldn't help Rusty not miss his father, but he could try to make the next five minutes more comfortable. "That's cool. Are ya any good?"

Rusty shrugged.

They pulled into the high school parking lot, and Blake drove toward a parking place.

"You don't need to come in. Dad usually just drops me off," Rusty said flatly, offering no room to consider any other option.

Blake tried anyway. "I don't mind. I'd like to see you play."

"No, really. It'll just make me uncomfortable. Can you just drop me off in the front of the school and pick me up after practice, like Dad did?"

Blake felt funny agreeing to just leave him at the school, and he had lied about Dave. Dave had said that he watched every practice. Maybe Rusty didn't want to have to explain why his father wasn't there. Blake could respect that. "Sure, no problem. What time should I come back?" Blake pulled up to the front of the school.

"Eight thirty." Rusty climbed out of the car, and before leaving, he leaned back in. "Thanks." He pressed his lips together, then said under his breath, "I really appreciate it."

Blake watched Rusty walk in the front doors of the school and wondered what he'd do for the next hour and twenty minutes. A bar was out of the question. Going home made no sense. By the time he got home, it would be almost time to come back and pick up Rusty. He settled on parking in the lot and surfing the Internet on his phone and maybe closing his eyes for a minute or two.

Parked under a tree in the side lot, Blake thought about his first appointment with Dr. Snow—*Danica*. She'd tamed her curly hair and pulled it away from her face. He noticed the telltale signs of attraction, the way she'd stared at his arms a second too long; then, in the next breath, she'd snapped into therapist mode. He liked that about her, that serious, smart side. It had taken all of his willpower not to stare at her long legs and the way her hair exposed the smooth skin of her neck. He'd looked down, out the window, anywhere but toward her magnificent body. He really wanted to change, but he wondered if he could reveal his darker, shameful side to a beautiful woman. To *that* beautiful woman? What choice did he have, really? A male therapist? That would be no better. He'd feel like he was bragging, whereas with a female, she'd surely have motivation to set him straight. No woman condoned a womanizer. Even those he hooked up with had hoped for more, and some had even laid into him when they'd seen him again and he hadn't called, as promised. He was beginning to understand the anger behind those vicious attacks. He'd caused them emotional pain, and they had just been giving it right back.

Blake looked up and watched a group of kids walking across the street, all wearing dark, hooded sweatshirts, hunched forward against the cold night's air. He stared for a few minutes, then realized that the one in the middle looked a lot like Rusty.

He pulled out of the parking lot and drove slowly by the group of kids, looking back in his side mirror. *Damn it to hell, Rusty*. Anger thundered in Blake's chest. He wasn't sure if he should approach him or let him be. What would Dave do? He pulled over around the corner and realized that he had no idea what Dave would do. Was he that bad of a friend? Shouldn't they have talked about these things? The ups and downs of Dave's family, not just Blake's conquests? *Damn it*. What would his own dad have done?

Blake stepped from the car and headed around the corner and up the sidewalk toward Rusty.

Rusty stopped in his tracks. His friends looked from him to Blake.

"Practice canceled?" Blake asked.

"Who is this dude?" the shortest kid asked.

Rusty put his palm out toward the kid. "No," he said to Blake.

"Dude? What practice?" another kid asked.

Blake looked at the five of them and was slow on the uptake. There was no practice. This was what Rusty did to get out with his friends. *Shit*. Blake may not have known much about parenting, but he knew it wasn't okay for a kid to ditch an adult or lie about where he was going and what he was doing. Why the hell would Dave have lied about going to the practices?

"Rusty? Do you want to talk in private?" Blake asked, trying to spare him from embarrassment.

"No," he said; then he spun on his heels. "Let's go."

"Whoa." Blake stood in front of him, arms crossed. "Rusty, I'm responsible for you. I can't just let you walk away." He leaned in closer, speaking quietly. "What would your dad have thought?"

"My dad? Shit, my dad didn't give a fuck about me or anyone else besides himself. He left me here and took off every week." Rusty barreled past him, his friends in tow.

What the hell was going on? Blake froze, watching his best friend's son walk away, going God knows where. Should he stop him, confront him again? Call Sally? Shit. He had no idea what to do, so he watched Rusty walk away, went back to his car, and parked in the school parking lot, asking himself why the hell he was wasting his time.

Blake pulled out his cell phone and dialed Danica's office number. If anyone had answers, it was a therapist, and she seemed smart and tactful. As expected, the answering machine came to life.

"This is Blake Carter. Thanks for seeing me today. I definitely would like to come back next week, if you're willing to see me. Please let me know."

At eight thirty on the dot, Rusty came back and climbed into the car. He just slumped down in the passenger seat and stared out the window. Blake inhaled deeply, waiting for the smell of cigarettes or marijuana to waft his way. There was no smell, which immediately made Blake worry that maybe Rusty was into something even more dangerous.

"Rusty?"

Rusty looked over. His eyes were clear, his jaw clenched, the muscles working against his teeth. Blake was looking into the face of a boy who was used to getting away with things.

"Wanna talk?" Blake asked.

"Not really," he answered, keeping eye contact with Blake.

This kid has balls. "Do I have to worry about you doing drugs?"

"No, I'm not doing drugs," Rusty said with attitude. "I'm not out stealing or pulling shit I shouldn't be pulling, okay?" He turned and looked out the front window. "Thanks for waiting."

Blake fought the desire to put him in his place. But his father had just died, after all. Maybe he needed to cut him some slack. Then again...

"Listen, I don't know what went on between you and your dad, but I'm nobody's slave, got it? If I drive you somewhere, I need to know where you're going, not where I'm dropping you off. You wanna hang with your friends? Then let your mother know where you're going.

You wanna sit on the curb for three hours in the dark and pick your nose? Let your mother know. But there's no way in hell I'll be party to you walking the streets when I have no clue what you're up to."

Blake started the car and drove toward Sally's house as Rusty continued to stare out the window. They drove in silence.

Blake parked in front of the house and scribbled down his phone number. "Here. If you're ever in any trouble." He shrugged. He didn't want to force himself on Rusty, but he wanted Rusty to know he was there for him. He handed it over.

Rusty held steadfast to the door handle, but he didn't move toward getting out of the car. He held the paper in his fist. "He's not who you thought he was, you know." He climbed out of the car and slammed the door.

Goddamnit. Who the hell does that kid think he is? Blake knew he had to talk to Sally, but he was in no mood for this shit tonight. And talking to Sally would just make him think about the shit Rusty had said about Dave. He checked his phone. No returned call from Danica. Weren't therapists, like doctors, supposed to be on call or something? The night just kept getting better and better.

Chapter Thirteen

By Sunday morning Danica had two new clients and a great idea of where to take Michelle. She threw on her jeans and a white, V-neck, cashmere sweater she'd had for years. She laced up her white Converse sneakers, which she'd purchased ages ago with Kaylie but had never worn. She eyed her Nine West pumps. It was a step, trying to define a line between work and her social life, even if a small one. She'd never wear sneakers to work. She wrapped a royal-blue scarf around her neck and grabbed her father's old army jacket, which she loved. On her way out the front door, she glanced in the mirror. She turned, inspecting herself from head to toe. She touched her hair, then her hips. *Not half bad.* There was something to be said about dressing young. For once her hair looked like it belonged on the person wearing it. Danica wondered why she didn't dress like that more often. A simple scarf and tossing away the pea coat for her father's jacket gave her a whole different outlook, and she felt it all the way down to her toes as she walked to the car with a new bounce in her step.

Michelle met her in her grandmother's foyer, wearing all black, straight down to the black Converse. Inside, Danica felt like a kid. She wanted to jump up and hug Michelle, squealing, *Look, I've got on Converse too!* Instead, she said, "Ready to go?"

Michelle surveyed Danica's outfit and smiled, then nodded.

"I'll bring her back by three, Nola," Danica said.

Michelle's grandmother took Danica's hand. "Bless you, Danica. You are a gift to her right now."

"Thank you. She's as much a gift to me."

Michelle rolled her eyes and walked out the door.

Danica drove to the Village, someplace she rarely went, although when she'd first moved back to Allure after college, she'd been sure she would spend a lot of time there. She'd imagined romantic strolls and dinners looking out at the mountains. But after she'd moved, real life had taken over, and those fantasies were just hopes that she would not let herself entertain, and she had quickly tucked them away. Until now.

She parked on the street in front of Steam, a little café with a line out the door. All of the Village streets were paved with bricks. Brick and stone town houses served as storefronts and restaurants. Ornate, iron fences and black, iron poles hosting old-fashioned lanterns lined the narrow streets. Danica sat in the driver's seat and remembered how she'd fallen in love with the Village. The Village had been Kaylie's hangout when they were growing up. Danica had hung out at the library. It wasn't until she had graduated from college and moved back home that she'd ventured to the Village again and become infatuated with its unique beauty.

"Are we getting out?" Michelle asked.

Danica grabbed her purse and opened the door. "We sure are."

They walked up the sidewalk.

"I've been here once," Michelle said.

"Really? Was it long ago?"

"Yeah. With my mom, when I was just a kid. Five, maybe? I don't remember exactly when, but I remember the bricks and the lights at night."

"It sounds like a good memory." *Don't sound like a therapist.* "I mean, the lights must have been lovely."

"Mm-hmm. I think we sat over there." She pointed to a courtyard. "There were fireworks, but I don't think it was the Fourth of July."

"They do fireworks here the second and last Friday of each month during the summers. I don't know if they did it back then, but maybe it was the same thing."

"Maybe."

They strolled past a tobacco shop, a candy shop, and another coffee shop.

"There it is." Danica pointed to a door with a decorative, wooden sign hanging above that read,

"Jewels of the Past." Danica had heard about the shop and sought it out for just this reason.

"What is it?"

"Vintage stuff." The cool air and her youthful clothing invigorated Danica. She grabbed Michelle's hand and pulled her up three brick steps and into the store. Incense filled the air. Wind chimes and festive decorations hung from the ceiling. Shelves lined the walls, filled with vintage clothing, books, and knickknacks. A bejeweled woman came out from behind the cash register. Bracelets gleamed halfway up her forearm.

"How are you ladies today? Welcome to a little piece of heaven." Her deep, brown eyes danced with a spark of energy. Her hair was cut above her shoulders, and like Danica's, was a mass of dark, natural curls gone haywire.

Danica was reeled in by her warm, wide smile. "I love your shop!" Danica exclaimed. From the eclectic feel to the earthy aroma, the shop reminded Danica of her college dorm. In college, her room had been filled with posters and knickknacks. She'd had interesting, mismatched furniture and even a little tree branch that she'd used to hang her necklaces on. She wondered what her condo smelled like to strangers. She'd have to pay more attention to that. She thought of her perfectly organized house, with the banana holder, place mats, and matching furniture right down to the bathroom trash can. She had the odd feeling that she'd become stodgy and she'd let her condo become stodgy, too. Boy, had she changed.

Michelle touched each box in a set of what looked like three shiny, smooth logs with intricate lines and hidden tops. She picked one up and flipped it open, then gasped. "Danica, you *have* to see this."

Was that excitement in her voice?

"My son makes those," the woman said proudly. "He lives in Canada on a small communal farm with my two grandbabies." She put a hand on Michelle's shoulder and watched her run her delicate finger along the edge of the smooth bark.

"Those are lovely." Danica looked inside. Atop a red velvet interior was a miniscule sculpture of a tree; tiny jewels hung from slivers of limbs made from copper wire.

"I can't believe your son makes these." Michelle set the smallest box down and picked up the next one in line. "They're so cool."

"He's pretty talented. But, then again, I am his mother." The woman leaned against a cabinet. Her plump behind stretched her blue, cotton pants. "You have the most beautiful eyes. How old are you? Fourteen? Fifteen?"

"Almost fifteen." Michelle shook her head, skillfully maneuvering her bangs into her eyes.

"I love your style, too. Have you ever thought about adding a splash of something to your dark aura?"

Aura?

The woman snagged a multicolored scarf from the branch of a display tree and placed it gently around Michelle's shoulders, carefully lifting her hair and draping the scarf down her chest. "You are gorgeous!"

Danica's jaw dropped open. Was it that easy? She could have just reached out and done what a mother might have? Or a cool aunt? Envy squeezed its fingers around her heart as she watched the woman chat easily with Michelle. Danica worried about every word that left her lips. Was it the right one? Did she sound too much like a therapist? Would she tip off a bad memory?

The woman was a blur of activity, moving from the scarf to the counter, where she chose a long necklace that had a flattened piece of tin on the end imprinted with overlapping moons, stars, and flowers around the edges, creating a frame around the word "imperfect." There was a fingernail-sized green charm that hung over the top. Danica held her breath, worried that Michelle would take offense to the statement.

Michelle lifted her finger and touched the necklace. She glanced at Danica from under her bangs.

Danica sighed and refrained from telling Michelle how the green in the scarf made her eyes pop, or how the addition of the simple necklace made her ninja outfit suddenly appear feminine and unique. She knew Michelle wanted her reaction, but she was afraid to say too much and scare her off. Instead Danica crossed her arms, her right hand drifting over her heart. Michelle looked like someone every teen girl would be envious of—tough and soft in the same breath. "It's just beautiful," she said.

The woman took Michelle's hand and guided her to a mirror; then she pulled Michelle's hair from around her face and set the thick of it down behind her shoulders.

Michelle stepped closer to the mirror, stroking the scarf, touching the necklace. Then she leaned in even closer, inches from the mirror, as if she didn't recognize her own face. She lifted her eyes and caught Danica's attention. She bit her lower lip and wrinkled her brow.

"Oh, Michelle. Look at you." Danica stood behind her, watching Michelle in the mirror. She was delighted with Michelle's new look, but she knew better than to fawn over her—anything she said might cause Michelle to say, *Whatever*, roll her eyes, and walk away.

Michelle turned to the woman and hugged her. Hugged her!

The woman laughed. "Oh, sweetie, you're welcome."

"Do you like it?" Michelle asked Danica.

"Do I? Michelle, you look like a million bucks. Cool and confident, but not like those snotty girls who spend hours getting ready." *Good, that was good, right?*

Michelle's lips spread into a smile, then faded. She unwrapped the scarf and handed it back to the woman. "Thank you. That's really pretty, but I don't have enough money to buy it."

"Well, that's okay, hon. You know it's here." The woman glanced at Danica as Michelle turned her back.

Danica nodded, indicating that she'd buy them.

The woman smiled.

Michelle removed the necklace and held it in her palm. "This is so...me."

The woman placed her hand beneath Michelle's and wrapped her fingers around the necklace. "It's yours."

Michelle's eyes grew wide. "What? No. I can't take this. Thank you, but..." She shot a look at Danica.

Danica was so happy for Michelle that a lump formed in her throat.

"Listen to me. It's rare that someone like you comes in. I mean, lots of high schoolers come in, filled with piss and vinegar," the woman waved her hands around, "talking too loud and not taking the time to really see what they're looking at. Something tells me that you see the beauty in owning what makes us each special."

Danica took out her wallet and paid for the scarf.

"Danica, no. I can't let you do that," Michelle pleaded.

Danica put her arm around Michelle and pulled her into her side. "I'm your Big Sister, right? I want to do this."

"Are you sure?" she asked, her eyes shining with delight.

"One hundred percent."

Throughout lunch, Michelle touched the scarf and ran the necklace through her fingers, almost as if she were afraid they might disappear. Danica noticed Michelle sitting up straighter, walking taller, and the smile that had been so rare last week had remained consistent all afternoon as they meandered through more of the shops.

In the car on the way back to her grandmother's house, Michelle clenched the ends of the scarf.

"Do you think I look stupid?" Michelle asked.

"Stupid? No, just the opposite." Danica shot her a smile.

"I felt great when we were in the Village, but now I'm worried everyone at school will, I don't know... think I look stupid, like I'm trying to be something I'm not." Michelle looked down at her lap.

Danica pulled up in front of Nola's house and turned in her seat to face Michelle. "I know what you mean."

"You do?" Michelle's eyes pleaded for understanding.

"Yeah. When I got dressed this morning, I felt young, maybe even a little bit cool. But now, as we head back toward town, I feel a little...I don't know...wrong, maybe? I'm so used to dressing more professionally that it feels funny to be so comfortable."

"I do love your sneakers and jacket," Michelle admitted.

Yes! "Really?"

"Uh-huh. You look great, not so...stuffy."

They both laughed.

"Yeah, not so stuffy. That's exactly how I feel. In fact, I like it so much that I'm going to try to dress a little more like this every day. I like how I feel when I wear this. My whole outlook is different."

"You totally should."

"Michelle." Danica reached for her hand, then thought better of it and pulled back. "My sister said something to me that really rang true, and I think it will for you, too. We don't have to be who our parents or people around us expect us to be."

"You have a sister?"

"Yeah." Danica smiled, thinking how odd it was for someone not to know Kaylie. "A beautiful, fun, outgoing, treacherously risky, younger sister."

Michelle laughed.

"Anyway, what my sister meant was that we don't have to live up to the expectations of others."

"What do you mean? You always tell me to be the best person I can be. So does Grandma."

"Yes, you should be the best person you can be. That's not really what I was referring to. Let me give you an example. All my life, I've been seen as the smart one, the responsible sister. And everyone saw my sister as the creative one, like that's all they expected of her. She was allowed to be less...I don't know. Academic, I guess. But with me, they expected the bookworm, the college graduate." Danica thought of her inability to separate who she was at work from who she was at home. "The conformist. So, that's who I am, and I'm trying to figure out if that's who I am because of what was expected, or if it's what I really wanted."

"And?"

Danica sighed. "I don't know. I just realized this recently, and I'm only in the thinking stage. But don't you see? This relates to you, too."

"Yeah, I'm totally not the bookworm, so I don't think so," Michelle joked.

"That's not what I mean. With you, everyone expects you to be the—for lack of a better word—the damaged girl, and I don't mean that you are damaged. What I mean is—"

"I know just what you mean." Michelle turned her body to face Danica. "I'm that girl! I live it. Everyone looks at me like there's something pitiful about me because of my mom or because I live with my grandma. It's like, my normal is their pity. Is that what you mean?"

Danica could not believe she was having this discussion in such a calm, meaningful fashion. She expected a snippy retort, a teenage rolling of the eyes. "Yes, that's exactly what I mean. And you don't have to be that person if you don't want to."

Michelle looked down, fingering the fringe on the scarf. "I kinda do. I mean, I am damaged."

Danica touched Michelle's hand. "No, you're not. Your mother is damaged, not you. Your grandmother is a sweet woman doing the best she can to raise a teenager. It's not you who is damaged, Michelle. It's what you were born into. I won't say you're perfect, because that would be a lie."

"You hate lies."

"Yup." Danica smiled, pleased that Michelle understood this about her. She'd been lied to only once by Michelle. When they first began the Big Sister program, Michelle hadn't called Danica to cancel an outing, and when Danica had shown up to pick her up, Michelle had lied and said she'd left a message. Danica had made no bones about her requirement of honesty, and Michelle had never lied to her again. "I do hate lies. The truth is, we're all imperfect. Those girls in your class who think you are a pariah are just scared. What if their moms had trouble? What would they do? How would they cope? See, you scare them because your situation makes them think."

Michelle squinted, nodded. "I guess I can see that."

"I don't want to lecture you. Just know that you aren't damaged. You don't have to fit into that square that everyone wants to put you in. You can wear your colors proudly, wear your necklace, and own your imperfections. Because, Michelle, that is more attractive than the fear those other kids are wearing." *Now, if only I could take my own advice.*

Chapter Fourteen

Monday morning rolled in with a flurry of snow and blustery wind. Blake rolled out of bed and walked groggily to the bathroom. He leaned over the sink wearing nothing but a pair of black Calvin Klein boxer briefs. His lean, muscular body moved stiffly. He stretched his arms above his head, gearing himself up for returning to AcroSki; Dave's absence had settled into his bones and muscles like a dull ache.

He splashed cold water on his face, then patted it dry with a towel, mentally ticking off his agenda for the day: Coffee and egg whites, open the store, more coffee. He wondered if he'd see Danica at the coffee shop. A hint of a thrill ran though his chest. He lifted his lips into a smile. He'd made it through the night without the company of a woman and without falling apart. That had to be a good sign. He'd take things day by day. He wondered if, while he was working out of his womanizing ways, he'd be like a heroin addict, begging to get laid.

He had an appointment with Danica later that morning. *Dr. Snow, off limits,* he reminded himself. After seeing her, he would call Sally and talk about Rusty. He felt guilty for not telling her about his ditching sooner, but every time he picked up the phone, he remembered Dave's recollection of the basketball practices. Something wasn't right, and he didn't want to open a can of worms he couldn't handle. He hoped Danica would have solid advice on how to handle that situation.

He turned on the shower and pulled off his boxers, flexing his thighs reflexively. Feeling the tension build, then release. He repeated it again, enjoying the rush of adrenaline as his muscles came to life.

He continued his daily to-do list: Hire someone to do some of the work that Dave handled, and think about finding a hobby. *A hobby. What was there besides women and skiing?* He'd wondered, right after the accident, if he'd ever ski again; then he'd quickly realized that skiing was not something he'd ever want to give up, and he was sure Dave wouldn't have wanted him to, either. He'd certainly take more care and fewer risks. He couldn't ski every day. He had quickly adapted to that change in lifestyle when he'd gone from being a ski instructor to owning a ski shop. He'd given up a lot of freedom, but it had been the right thing to do. Financial freedom was *not* overrated.

He stepped into the shower and stood beneath the flow of water, letting it roll down his face and back. He closed his eyes, feeling the strain in his muscles ease. Blake turned around and set his palms on the ceramic shower wall. The water beat the tension from between his shoulder blades.

One day at a time. He could do this.

AcroSki came to life at ten o'clock. After Alyssa, the part-time employee, showed up, Blake set a sign on the counter in the hopes of avoiding multiple inquiries about Dave. It read: *Dave Tuft, co-owner of AcroSki, passed away this past weekend. He will be deeply missed. Please send condolences to...*" followed by the address of the church Sally attended. Blake longed to hear Dave's taunts and stories about his family-filled weekend, although now Blake wondered how much of them were true.

Blake had looked over the files on Dave's desk and realized just how much Dave had taken care of. They'd been so in sync with each other that dividing and conquering had become natural. Now he'd have to sort out the dealings of the inventory, accounting, and staff schedules. Anxiety prickled his spine. He needed a few minutes to regroup before he dove into Dave's desk.

"I'm gonna grab a coffee. Would you like one?" he asked Alyssa.

Tall and lean, with a skier's muscular build, Alyssa turned her ponytailed head in his direction. "Nah, I'm cool. Go ahead. I've got this."

Blake headed out the door. He'd been disappointed when he didn't see Danica at the coffee shop before work. He braced himself against the cold and headed there again.

The aroma of coffee reminded him of the morning he'd accidentally struck Danica. He laughed to himself. *It is a small world.* Three women looked up from their table, their eyes devouring him like he was a giant chocolate bar. He took his place in the back of the line.

The line moved quickly, and when it was his turn, the familiar barista said, "Hiya, Blake. The usual?"

"Yeah, sure." He thought about it, then said, "No, wait. How about a vanilla latte instead, and a bagel with cream cheese."

"Wow, bring it on," she joked.

Change is good. Blake hadn't eaten a bagel in what felt like years. He stuck to a strict diet of coffee, protein, veggies, alcohol, and—of course—women. He took the bag and cup from the barista, paid, and headed back out into the snow. He walked with his head down, shoulders hunched against the wind, rethinking the bagel.

The door to AcroSki pulled from his hands with the weight of the wind. He tugged it shut behind him and wiped the snow from his shoulders.

"It's a cold one, huh?" Alyssa said.

"I brought you something." He took off his parka and made his way to the office. He set the coffee down and handed Alyssa the bagel. He was already tackling changing his personal habits; changing his eating habits would have to wait.

"I don't need this," she said, then patted her stomach.

"Please." He laughed. "Carb load. You'll need it today, to pick up the pieces of Dave's—of the work we need to get done." His heart ached as the spark in Alyssa's eyes dimmed.

"Right," she said, and walked away, bagel in hand. The door closed behind her, leaving Blake alone in the office he and Dave had shared, alone with his thoughts, memories, and fears. He sat in the chair and stared at the desk. There were signs of Dave everywhere, from the picture of his family to the scribblings on the calendar and the sticky notes placed haphazardly on the wall.

Blake leaned forward and put his forehead to his hands. He closed his eyes and took a deep breath. Focus. *What would Dave do?* That was the problem. He'd known Dave for years, and yet he had no idea what he might do in this situation. Rusty's voice picked at his mind. *"My dad didn't give a fuck about me or anyone else besides himself."*

"Dave, what the hell was going on?" he said to the empty room.

There was a feeling of submissiveness that went along with seeing a female therapist, and being submissive was not something Blake was comfortable with. He sat across from Danica, reminding himself that it was his choice to be there. It didn't help. He still felt like a high school kid in the principal's office. A beautiful principal's office.

"What would you like to talk about today, Blake? Do you feel ready to talk about Dave?"

Blake ran his eyes over Danica's crazy hair, down her shirt and slacks, trying to figure out what looked different.

"Are you done?" she asked, glaring at him, her eyebrows lifted.

"I'm sorry. I wasn't looking at you like *that*." Blake wiped his face with his hand, wondering if he *was* looking at her like that.

"Like what?" she asked.

"You know, like guys look at women. You look different today, and I was trying to figure out what it was."

Danica smiled. "Okay, thanks for noticing."

"Ha!" he said loudly. "I knew something was different. But, honestly, I have no clue what it is."

Danica shook her head. "That's okay. We're not here to talk about my clothing. Dave, remember?"

Blake took a deep breath and crossed his arms. "Dave. Right." *Where do I begin?* "I took Dave's son, Rusty—he's fifteen—to his basketball practice the other day. Well, I thought I was taking him to basketball practice, but he snuck out with his friends and I caught him."

"That's not so strange for a teenager." Danica wrote something on her notepad.

"No, but...where do I start?" *Just tell her. Lay it all out on the line.* "Okay, here's the thing. Dave used to talk about going to his basketball practices each week and about how great their family life was, but according to Rusty, Dave never went to his practices."

"Ah, I see. Dave lied to you. How does that make you feel?" Danica sat back and watched Blake, her gaze never wavering from his eyes.

Blake's nerves tightened in his chest. "That's not really what's bothering me. Most people pretend to have much better lives than they really have, I think. Everyone embellishes something." Blake fidgeted with his hands, then leaned forward, unnerved by Danica's silence. He looked up at her again and realized that it was her jacket that was different. The last time he'd seen her she was perfectly tailored, head to toe. Today she wore a flowing, cotton batik jacket with what looked like a cotton camisole underneath. On someone else it might make them look frumpy. Danica looked anything but frumpy.

Blake sat up and said, "I think what's bothering me is that this guy was my best friend, but I really didn't know him. I mean, we had the business together—he did his thing and I did mine, and we skied together. But when it came to knowing what he'd do in certain situations, or what he had going on in his life on any deeper level, I have no clue. I mean, Rusty said his dad didn't give a fu—" Blake caught the word before he finished. "Sorry. He said Dave didn't give a damn about him or anyone else, and that's not at all the guy I knew. The Dave I knew adored his family."

"Sometimes a teenager's perception is skewed by something they're experiencing in their lives. He may have seen his father's attention as prying, a pain in the rear."

Blake thought about that. "Yeah, I guess so, but he said Dave didn't go to the practices, either."

"Well, teenagers are all about the here and now, so maybe Dave had missed the last few practices, or maybe he never went at all. Would that have changed things between you and Dave?"

"No, not between us, but it means he might have lied to me."

"And how does that make you feel? How do you think you could have changed that? Could you have done anything so he wouldn't have lied to you?"

"I don't know. I could have asked him questions, talked to him more."

"Probably, but was that who you were in the relationship? You see, Blake, I think we all serve a role in every relationship. Sometimes we're the aggressor, sometimes the center of attention; sometimes we're there for show, like a trophy wife, if you will. Other times, though, we might be the person who builds others up, or the one who needs building up. We can't be everything in every relationship." Danica set her notepad down on the desk. "You know, sometimes friendships are not the kind to share the more difficult aspects of our lives; but that more superficial friendship—or, just sharing the happier moments—doesn't mean it was any less valuable. I think sometimes it makes them more valuable. Maybe that's the type of friendship the two of you shared. Maybe he felt like he could be this other person with you, the one with no trouble brewing."

"But I think most people are a little bit of all those things." Blake leaned forward, paying close attention to what she said.

"Sometimes people can be, yes, but if all those aspects of their personality are not already present, they can't really fake it very well. So you have to ask yourself, who were you in your relationship with Dave?"

Blake sat back again and crossed his arms. *I was the guy he egged on, the one he envied. I was the guy who made jokes and banged women.* "I don't think I was a very good friend."

"That's a pretty harsh judgment. Were you the friend Dave needed? Was he the friend you needed?"

She was looking at him again in that way that tied his stomach into knots, like she expected an insightful answer that Blake didn't know how to give. "How can I know that?" he asked.

"Well, did you feel as though your friendship was lacking something when Dave was alive, or are you just feeling that way now? Grief can manifest in many ways, and it can skew our memories."

Damn, you're good. Was he skewing his memories of their relationship? "I think we had a good relationship.

We enjoyed our time together—I enjoyed our time together. I can't really know if Dave did."

"No, you can't, and you can't change the type of friend you were to Dave, though I'd imagine you weren't a bad friend. Most people don't hang around with people they don't enjoy." Danica lifted her pen to her lips. *Oh, those lips.* "Blake, is there a chance that Dave's death is making you question what kind of a friend you are in general? I mean to others, not just Dave?"

He crossed his arms.

Danica set her pen on the desk and leaned back in her chair. "You look like a bundle of hot wires ready to short out. What are you thinking right this second? What are you not saying?"

Anger squeezed his muscles tighter.

"I'm prying, and I realize that. But, Blake, I'm not sure this is about not knowing Dave as much as it might be about something bigger, like maybe not knowing yourself very well."

Blake let out a breath and said, "Okay, yeah. I don't have other friends. There, okay? That's it. I'm not a guy who people hang out with. I'm a guy women sleep with and who guys have a random beer with, or ski with, or look at like I'm some kind of magical creature because I can sleep with as many women as I want." His cheeks felt like they were on fire. He was a caged lion in need of escape. He stood and paced next to the window, pissed off that she could sit so calmly while his insides were fuming. "Is that what you want to hear?" *Bitch.*

"This isn't about me." She sounded like a teacher, a principal, a parole officer.

"Right. Maybe I made a mistake coming here." He ran his hand through his hair, then crossed his arms, staring out the window.

"That's completely up to you."

"You sit there like you're high and mighty, like you don't ever do shit that makes you feel like a bad person." He spun around and looked at Danica, sitting with her legs crossed, leaning against the back of the chair. She looked calm, cool, and collected, while his anger simmered to a boil.

"I'm sorry you feel that way. We all do things that make us feel inadequate, and it's totally normal to get mad when we realize things we'd rather not see in ourselves."

"Oh, so now I'm inadequate?" he seethed.

"No." She smiled, but her eyes betrayed her. They said something akin to, *Of course you are.*

Blake crossed his arms and stared at her, this time waiting for her to finish speaking. Putting her on the spot.

"What I'm saying is that if you don't like who you were with Dave, you can't change that, but you can change those things you don't like about yourself with regard to friendships, or anything else for that matter."

Blake grabbed his jacket from the hook and said, "I think we've talked enough for today."

Danica stood, her lips slightly parted, her face soft, her eyes sweetly empathetic. "That's fine. This is your session."

Blake had a sudden urge to take her in his arms and kiss the high and mighty out of her. She was as sexy as she was infuriating. Blake walked to the door and reached for the handle. "Thank you."

When she spoke, her voice was confident and strong, "Blake, therapy is hard. Things usually get worse before they get better."

He turned to face her, one hand on his escape route, the other clutching his jacket.

"You're not here because you're perfect. You're here because you wanted to deal with something. We're dredging up those things that may not be what you want to know about yourself. Think of your mind like a garden. We're tilling the soil, bringing the buried stuff up to the surface—the mucky, hard, rotting, forgotten things that have been hidden for probably far too long. This is the hard part. Seeing it for what it is."

Blake didn't know what else to say. Even though anger twisted and yanked at his muscles, he knew she was right.

"It gets easier. I promise."

He walked out the door without a word.

Chapter Fifteen

Shit! It had been hours since his therapy session with Danica and Blake still couldn't shake the tension that tugged at every nerve in his body. He sat on a bar stool, nursing his fourth Jack and Coke, checking out the eye candy. Most women who drank at five in the afternoon were either waiting for a pack of noisy girlfriends or lonely old women hoping to feel young again. Blake wasn't sure he cared which kind of woman he left the bar with, as long as he didn't leave alone. He'd show *her* just how inadequate he was.

Pickings were sparse at Bar None. The redhead in the corner had been eye-raping him for the past hour. He found redheads to be aggressive, which he normally loved, but this time his ego needed a long, luscious stroke. Playful and hot, that would do it. He lifted his eyes to ESPN playing on the television above the bar.

"Imagine meeting you here."

Blake turned around to find Kaylie's firm breasts at eye level. The right side of his lips lifted into a smile. "It's the only bar in town where tourists don't flock. You look like that and that's the line you choose?" He laughed.

Kaylie climbed onto the stool next to him, swinging her knees toward him. Her dark blue miniskirt barely covered what Blake imagined she wore beneath: a lacy thong.

She leaned toward him. The want in her eyes unveiled. "Buy me a drink?"

He lifted his glass in the direction of the older, male bartender.

"What'll it be?" the bartender asked with a husky voice while he looked lasciviously at Kaylie.

Blake leaned possessively toward her.

"I'll have what he's having," Kaylie answered. She twirled her hair around her index finger. "What are you doing here?" she asked Blake. "Isn't it a bit early for all this?" She pointed to the empty glasses lined up beside him.

"Tough afternoon." Blake could not take his eyes off of the crest of her breasts, peeking out of her tight, white, V-neck shirt.

"Yeah? Tell me about it. I just got back in town from a wild concert. I'm whipped." She took a drink. "That hits the spot."

"Are you meeting someone here?" Blake looked around the bar, remembering the guy she'd left with the last time he'd seen her.

"Nah." She swatted her hand through the air. "I was supposed to meet my sister, but she just called and gave me some lame excuse about a hard day at work. So," she shrugged, "I figured I'd come in, relax awhile, then go home."

"Sounds good to me." Blake lowered his lids and leaned in close when he spoke. *I've still got it.*

Kaylie giggled. "Yeah? Okay then." She downed the drink and held up the glass, asking for another. "So, tell me, Blake," she over pronounced the *B*, giving his name a forceful tone, "why was your day so tough? Didn't sell many skis?"

Blake finished his drink in one gulp, thinking about Danica and her smug look as he opened up to her. "Just a painful meeting. Nothing to worry your pretty, little head about." The last thing he wanted to do was think about Danica. Blake considered ordering one more drink, but he knew he was on the verge of dropping over the edge, and with Kaylie in his sights, he wanted to be on his game—for later.

"Ski shop owners have meetings?" She pressed her knee against his thigh.

"Of sorts," he said. He had nothing to do with his hands. Without a drink, he longed to do something with them. He draped his left arm around the back of her stool.

"Tell me what life is like for a ski shop owner. I would imagine that it's nothing but fun."

His fingertips brushed against her back, and she leaned into his hand. It was so easy for him. He could sleep with her in the next five minutes if he wanted. Hell, he could slip one hand up her skirt right now and she'd just wiggle so no one else could see. Blake felt the familiar desire in his groin, but his mind fell back to his session with Danica. *We all do things that make us feel inadequate.* Damn her. He dropped his arm from around Kaylie and ordered another drink.

"I just lost my business partner." Why the hell did he reveal that?

"Bummer. Did you guys have, like, a blowup? A disagreement?"

"He died." Blake took a swig of his drink.

"Jesus, I'm so sorry. That's awful." Kaylie put her hand on his leg.

Blake stared at her hand. He felt like the epitome of the quintessential man with a devil on one shoulder and an angel on the other, both whispering in his ear. "I miss him." *Jesus. Why am I telling* her *this?* He didn't want to think about going into AcroSki tomorrow, or the day after, or even the day after that, knowing Dave would never be there again.

"Aw, I'm sure you do. I can't imagine what that would be like."

Her words oozed empathy, and Blake's hard exterior fell away like a snake shedding its skin. "I can't even talk to his wife. I have no idea what to say to her." He had no idea what was happening to him. When had he developed diarrhea of the mouth—and worse, of his emotions? He looked at his glass. It had to be the alcohol. He ran his hand through his hair—a distraction from the heat beneath her palm.

"She probably just needs someone to tell her everything will be okay."

Blake wondered if it could be that easy.

"Seriously. I mean, you can't fix it for her, but you can be there, hug her, help her through by just being around."

"She won't want me around. I'm just a reminder that he's gone, and...I never really spent a lot of time with her. I mean, I had dinner with Dave and his family often enough, but I don't know." *I never spend any real time with anyone.*

She ran her index finger in circles on his thigh, downed her drink, and ordered another. "I can't imagine anyone not wanting you around." She licked her lips.

Blake looked at the mirror behind the bar. The image staring back at him was the image he'd seen in the bathroom mirror when he was with Red—a hungry, tired player who was hiding from the things that mattered in life, even if he wasn't quite sure what they were. He didn't want to be that person anymore, and yet there he was, on the prowl. He looked over at Kaylie's reflection, with her puppy-dog eyes, hanging on to his every word. Then he thought of his meeting with Danica and how she'd listened without trying to fix him. She'd just let him work through his emotions, bring them all out on the table. And she didn't judge him or tell him he was a shitty friend. *We all do things that make us feel inadequate. All* being the key word. And, he commended himself, he *was* trying to change.

Kaylie leaned in close and whispered, "Wanna go back to my place? I'll help you feel better."

"Absofuckinglutely," he said out of habit, but he didn't move.

Kaylie stood and reached for his hand.

She was gorgeous, willing, and certainly able, but if he went home with her, he'd be starting at square one. Blake imagined her naked body beneath him, the taste of her on his lips, and his desire intensified. He looked in the mirror again as he stood up. *Same guy, different day.*

He closed his eyes for a second, then turned to Kaylie and said, "I'm sorry, but I'm afraid I'm going to pass." *Shit. Can I really do this?*

Kaylie's jaw dropped open. "Excuse me?" She turned her head sideways, placing her ear closer to his mouth, like she hadn't heard him right.

"I'm sorry. You're gorgeous, you're great to talk to, but honestly, I'm dealing with some shit right now, and this," he moved his hand between them, "this won't help it any."

"What the hell is wrong with you?" Her cheeks flushed with anger.

"I have no idea." Blake turned back toward the bar. "But I'm trying to figure that out."

Sisters in Love

"You have issues, Blake. Jesus Christ. You need a shrink or something. First you turn me down the other night, and now you lead me on and—"

His heart ached when he saw the liquid anger in her squinted eyes. "It's not you, okay? It's me. I just can't do this anymore."

"My sister's a shrink. She can probably help you with your bullshit issues." Kaylie laughed.

Blake saw through her laugh to her hurt. "I'm sorry. You're right. I do have bullshit issues. Oh, and I already have a shrink."

"Yeah, well, Danica is probably ten times better." She grabbed her coat from the back of her stool and stomped out of the bar.

Danica? Her sister? Blake's pulse raced like he'd just dodged a bullet.

Chapter Sixteen

Pounding on the front door drew Danica's attention from the files she'd been reviewing.

"Danica!"

Kaylie. Danica opened the door and Kaylie flew past her in a rage. "I don't know what the hell is up with that guy, but Jesus Christ, if he keeps doing what he's doing, I'm gonna be the one on your couch."

Danica watched her sister storm around the room and flop onto the couch, sending her files to the floor. "Who did what this time?" She picked up the files and set them on the coffee table in front of Kaylie.

"Blake. The jerk. Remember him, from the bar? Didn't he call your practice, or come to see you or something?" Kaylie's face was red and her eyes were glassy. The way she slouched on the couch in her wrinkled miniskirt, she looked like a sullen teenager wronged by the quarterback.

She'd forgotten that she mentioned she'd seen Blake. At least she hadn't confirmed that he was her client—a fact she quickly decided was better left undisclosed. She skipped over Kaylie's question altogether. "Blake? As in Blake Carter? AcroSki? That jerk?" *What the hell?*

"Yeah, that jerk. I saw him at Bar None." She turned scornful eyes on Danica. "Thanks for that, by the way. If you hadn't stood me up, I probably wouldn't be having such a shitty night."

Danica picked up the files and placed Blake's on the bottom of the stack, then set them on the dining room table and sat next to Kaylie.

She let out a long sigh. "Let me guess. He was at the bar, but he went home with someone else?" *I knew today would set him back.*

"Yes. No. Shit. He didn't go home with someone else." Kaylie covered her face and screamed into her palms. When she brought her hands away, her anger had turned to disappointment. "He acted like he wanted to go home with me, and—"

"Wait." Danica stopped her. "What happened to Chad, or Chaz, or whatever his name was? Didn't you just get back from a weekend away with him?"

"Don't judge me, okay?"

Danica sat back against the pillows, reminding herself that Kaylie was her sister, not her client. "Fine. Go on."

"Chaz and I had a good time, but since I was going to meet you anyway, I went in for a drink. He was there, and...Jesus, well, you saw him. You really expect me to turn away from him?"

You bet your ass, I do. He's my client, even if he is challenging my ability to stay on the professional side of things.

She didn't give Danica time to answer. "Anyway, we were getting up to leave, and he said some bullshit about how he couldn't do it."

"Did he say why?" *What are you up to, Blake Carter?*

"He just lost his business partner—he died, if you can believe that."

"I can."

"And he said he doesn't know how to talk to the guy's wife."

Really? Danica made a mental note to explore Blake's discomfort with Dave's wife. She looked at the file and thought about telling Kaylie that Blake had become her client. That would end things right there. He'd be off the table immediately. Kaylie didn't date guys who had anything to do with therapists. She assumed anyone who needed therapy was severely broken and weak. If only she knew how therapy could help her with her man-juggling habits—and that Blake was seeking help for the very same reasons. But she could not reveal that he was a client. Danica respected her client's confidentiality, and Blake was no different, even if Kaylie had been hurt by him.

"Sounds like he's got a lot to deal with right now. Besides, why do you want someone other than Chad?"

"Chaz."

"Chaz," Danica repeated. Chaz could be Rick, Steve, Dean, or Carl, for all she cared. She didn't invest too much energy into Kaylie's men. They came and went faster than the wind changed direction.

Kaylie kicked her UGGs up onto the coffee table. Danica reached over and took her sister's boots off of her feet, then set them on the floor.

"Thanks," Kaylie said in her best little-girl voice. "Do you think it's me?" she asked.

"You? No. You said yourself that he's got stuff going on in his life, and it sounds like heavy stuff. I would steer clear of him." She had to get her off of the Blake track. He would do nothing but hurt her in the long run. Danica thought about that for a second, then decided that Kaylie was equally as capable of hurting him, especially in his current state. She'd seen men go through the great realization before: They weren't the man they thought they were; they drank too much, played around too much, ate too much, hated women, hated their mothers, hated life. She had a long way to go with Blake before she would understand his real issues, but there was one thing she did know. Breaking through and revealing his faults the way he had was painful for him, and now she also saw that it had had a tremendous impact. What he did with that knowledge over the next few weeks would prove whether he was capable of changing his behavior. More important, whether he really wanted to change.

Turning away from Barbie-doll Kaylie was a step in the right direction.

"What on earth are you wearing?" Kaylie asked with a laugh.

Danica looked down at her flowing jacket. "What? I like it. I took Michelle to the Village this weekend, and it made me realize that I dress like an old lady."

"It took a trip to the Village for you to realize that? You mean my constant reminding did nothing to tip you off?" She smiled and kicked her stockinged foot in Danica's direction.

"Do you like it?" she asked tentatively.

Kaylie assessed Danica's outfit. "Yeah, I do, even if it doesn't really match your slacks."

"What do you mean? Black matches everything." She looked down at her slacks.

"Usually that's true, but that jacket belongs with jeans and UGGs, not slacks and heels. You look like Cloris Leachman, or Maude, or one of those women."

"Really?" No wonder Blake had been looking at her that way. And there she was, feeling so confident in just another old-lady outfit.

Kaylie took Danica's hand and dragged her toward the stairs. "Come on, sis. I've been dying to give you a makeover for years." Kaylie ran up the stairs like a teenager ready to trade secrets.

Danica followed behind, sighing along the way.

Upstairs, in Danica's room, Kaylie passed the bed and said, "No Twizzlers?"

"A whole drawer full, unfortunately," Danica joked.

Kaylie rummaged through Danica's closet, pulling shirts and blouses down and tossing them at her. "Put these on the bed."

Danica sifted through the mismatched jackets, jeans, leggings, and shirts. She sat on the bed and watched Kaylie move from the closet to the dresser, weeding through Danica's jewelry and laying out necklaces and earrings across the top. She pulled open Danica's top drawer.

"Hey, no need to go in there," Danica said.

"Are you kidding me?" Kaylie dug through Danica's lingerie, withdrawing the laciest—and the most uncomfortable—bras and panties that Danica owned.

Danica watched, shaking her head.

"Never in your life have you let me help you with this," Kaylie said with her back to Danica.

"Well, maybe change is good."

Kaylie turned around. "Yeah, maybe it is." She came and sat down next to Danica. They both faced the mirror above the dresser. "Why do I do it?"

Danica tilted her head. "Because you love clothes and I have a very tenuous relationship with them."

"No, I don't mean that. I mean with guys. Chaz is so nice. He's really good to me, and he's definitely hot. So, why do I, you know, try to get other guys when I'm happy?"

Danica knew better than to answer.

"Come on. You're a therapist. Can't you help me?" Kaylie pleaded.

They stared at each other through their reflections. Danica leaned her head on Kaylie's. "You don't want my help, Kaylie."

"Maybe you're right," Kaylie said. "But I get it, you know? I know *you* think there's something wrong with what I'm doing."

"I don't judge you. I love you," Danica answered.

"Thank God someone does." Kaylie jumped up and began putting together outfits.

Danica's heart broke with the realization she so often had—that everyone carries baggage. Some people's was just lighter than others'.

Chapter Seventeen

Blake sat in his car in front of the funeral home, watching a drizzle of freezing rain cut through the dense fog. People filed into the low, brick building, heads down, umbrellas perched like shields. Nothing could shield Blake from the sting of the hours to come. Loneliness settled in around him. He'd be the only person walking in alone, which up until that very moment had never bothered him. He took pride in the way he could own an entrance. His looks and his confidence had served him well, but now there was nothing he'd like more than to be invisible.

When his cell phone rang, he stared at the number. *Danica Snow*. He picked it up, his voice tethered by sadness. "Hello?"

"Blake?"

"Yes, hi, Danica...um...Dr. Snow?" What an idiot. What was the protocol?

"Danica is fine. I'm looking over my schedule for next week and realized that you hadn't confirmed our Monday appointment. Rather than fill that slot, I thought I'd see if you were planning on coming in." The professionalism in her voice left no room for assumptions about her phone call.

"Yes, please."

"Okay. Would you like me to hold every Monday? Same time?"

Blake realized his disregard for her schedule and pulled himself out of his discomfort enough to apologize.

"It's not a problem this time, but if you could either set a day and time or let me know by Wednesday each week for the following week, that would be helpful."

Blake sighed. He'd fucked up again. When was he going to get his act together? "I'm sorry, Danica. Yes, please, every Monday would be great. Do you have time now, to talk, I mean?"

An uncomfortable silence passed between them, and Blake took the hint. "I don't mean personally. I'm outside of Dave's funeral. It's starting in ten minutes, and I'm not sure how...what to do. I'm uncomfortable."

"I can spare ten minutes. I'll just add the time to your next bill."

There it was. All business. "Thank you." Suddenly, Blake didn't feel so alone.

"Do you have a friend with you?" Danica asked. "Someone to walk in with?"

"Nope. Just me."

"Okay, well, remember, you are doing this because Dave was a friend, so this is not really about you. You are doing this for closure, but really, funerals are for showing support to the family."

"I never thought of it like that."

"I know. Most people are too absorbed with their own feelings or discomfort to look beyond, to the loved ones who were left behind."

Blake pictured Danica sitting behind her desk, pen in hand, her eyes full of compassion.

"Sally and Rusty will be happy you are there. You were his business partner, his friend. Even if you are grappling with that friendship, they need you there. You should be there, to honor and remember Dave."

Blake looked out the window at a young couple walking in. The man had his arm around the woman's shoulders, pressing her tight against him underneath the umbrella. He wondered if they felt as uncomfortable as he did. "Right. What does that mean exactly? What do I do? I'm not good at these things. I'm better in a bar." He mustered a little laugh.

Danica remained professional and direct. "Blake, you can do this. You are more than just a bar guy. Look in the mirror and tell me what you see. Right now. Go ahead."

Blake tilted the rearview mirror and looked at his face. What did he see? He felt stupid looking at himself and trying to describe what he saw. A handsome guy? A mourning friend? Nothing seemed right.

"Blake? Top of your head, stream of consciousness. Tell me what you see."

"I can't. I don't know what I see. A guy. A confused, sleazy guy." He turned the mirror away.

Danica sighed. "I thought you might see that. I know you just looked away from the mirror. Look again." She waited.

How the hell? He moved the mirror.

"I bet if you look deeply enough, you'll see the funny guy Dave saw. The confident, exciting, capable skier, the businessman and friend. He's in there. Do you see him?"

Blake felt himself smile. "Maybe." He was being snarky and he knew it. He got his feelings in check and said, "Okay, yeah, I can find that guy in there."

"Good. Now remove the thoughts about being sleazy. Confused is okay, but sleazy has no place at a funeral. Find that guy Dave loved and take him inside. Sit down midway, not up front, not in the back. Up front is assumptive, and back rows are for people who want to hide."

"Invisible would be good."

"No, it wouldn't. You respected Dave, and he respected you. Sit down, listen to the words, and let yourself feel what is said about your friend. Honor him with your attention—and your emotions. If you cry, it's okay. If you laugh, it's okay. If you feel something, then you've done a good job. That's all that's really important. This is about Dave's family, not about what you look like in there. Okay?"

The way she said, *Okay*, filled with compassion, made Blake's stomach lurch.

"Okay. I can try."

"I have faith in you, and I'll see you Monday."

Blake hit the End button on his phone and looked in the mirror again, searching his dark eyes for that person Danica seemed sure existed. *Do this for Sally and Rusty.* He climbed from the car and went into the building, searching for the appropriate middle row and settling in next to a painfully thin, gray-haired woman with skin that was almost translucent. She turned to him and smiled, though her greenish-gray, murky eyes were already tear-filled.

Blake nodded in acknowledgment. He looked around her and noticed that there was an empty space on her other side. It appeared that she was alone, too. Blake took comfort in that, then realized that taking comfort in her discomfort was probably not the right thing to do. His confidence faltered, and he reminded himself again of why he was there. *Sally and Rusty.*

The service moved swiftly and sadly through forty-five minutes of memories and meaningful passages from family members. The woman sitting next to him cried throughout. Blake tried his hardest to listen to every word, but in his mind danced images of Dave and their last day on the slopes. He should have seen his angst; he should have stopped him, demanded that they ski together. But that wasn't who Blake was. He'd been too wrapped up in his own thoughts to reach out, and now he'd lost him. *This is not about you*, he reminded himself. *Sally and Rusty lost him.*

After the service, Blake stepped from his seat and offered his hand to the older woman to help her up.

"Thank you," she said in a trembling voice. "I hate these services, and at my age, I'm going to them every week."

"Did you know Dave well?" Blake asked.

"Not really. I saw him coming and going from his car each week, but he was close with my neighbor, so I wanted to pay my respects." They headed toward the door.

"Is your neighbor here?" Blake asked.

"Yes, back row." She nodded toward a small, blond woman. "Poor dear. She's had a tough time of it. I don't know what she'll do now."

Blake didn't recognize the woman, though he wouldn't, he realized. Outside of a few ski buddies, he had no idea who Dave spent time with. According to Dave, not many people besides his family. But wouldn't she have sat with the family if she were close to them? He watched the woman pull on her heavy, wool coat and rush out of the building alone.

After the cemetery service, Blake approached Sally. He was glad he had the umbrella to hold on to. He needed something to focus on besides the fact that his best friend was being put into the ground. He wished Sally had waited until spring, giving them all time to accept Dave's passing. She'd been adamant about his immediate burial, and though he understood her need for closure, it didn't help alleviate the sick feeling in his stomach.

He hugged Sally. "I'm really sorry." He wondered if Sally blamed him, but dared not ask. He didn't really want to know the answer.

Sally nodded, unable to speak beyond her tears. She clung to him and cried. Blake held her, while Rusty watched him out of the corner of his eye. Blake knew Rusty worried that he'd tell Sally about him skipping practice. Even Blake knew this was not the time or place for such discussions. He winked at Rusty to ease his mind and watched the boy's worry slip into a relieved nod.

Sally pulled back from Blake, wiping her eyes.

"Dave would be glad you're here," she said.

Blake noticed that she didn't say she was glad he was there. *This is about his family, not you.* "He was a good man, Sally. I wish I could have stopped—"

Sally shook her head, fresh tears spilling down her cheeks. "Don't. You couldn't have stopped him. This was probably a long time coming."

"What do you..."

She leaned in close, out of Rusty's earshot. "There were problems between me and Dave." She searched his eyes, and Blake wondered if she saw his disbelief; then she continued. "We really need to talk."

Blake's voice failed him. Sally pursed her lips the way women do when they're holding back violent sobs. Her chest hitched. Blake shot a look at Rusty, who was now standing far away from them with his head bowed, facing the parking lot. *Dave, what was going on?*

"Sally...I didn't know," Blake began.

Sally shook her head, then looked at Rusty. "Don't. Sunday? Rusty is going to a friend's house for the afternoon. Can you come by around one?"

Blake felt like he was standing on the edge of the slopes, and one step in the wrong direction would send him tumbling over the cliff. *This is about Sally and Rusty, not me.* "Of course. Sure."

Chapter Eighteen

Michelle answered the door with teary eyes and a red nose Sunday morning. Danica's therapist senses perked up. "What's wrong?" She walked into the foyer.

"Grandma's sick," Michelle explained through tears.

"How sick? Is she here?" Danica looked around the small room, then glanced in the kitchen.

"She's in her bedroom." Michelle led Danica into the living room, where she sat on the sofa. Family photographs hung above a small fireplace. The carpet beneath their feet was golden and worn, the dingy color of mustard powder. A piano sat off to the side, with photographs of Michelle at all ages and ones of her mother as a younger woman.

"Michelle, is she okay? Should I take her to the hospital?" Danica waited for an explanation as Michelle sniffled and wiped her eyes.

She shook her head. "No, she doesn't have a fever or anything. She's just tired and has a sore throat."

Danica breathed a sigh of relief. "Thank goodness. You scared me. But why the tears? Is there something else going on?" She watched Michelle's face for signs of trouble, and beneath the tears, her cheeks trembled. "Michelle, what is it? You can tell me."

"It's just..." She swiped at her eyes. "It's stupid, I know, but...I can't help thinking...what if Grandma dies? Who will take care of me?"

Danica had worried about that herself. The truth was, Michelle had no other family members to turn to. She'd likely go into the foster system until she was eighteen...unless her mother could pull her shit together.

"You can't think like that. Your grandmother is not old, by any means, and a cold is hardly something to worry about."

Michelle grabbed a tissue and blew her nose. "I knew you wouldn't understand." She stood and walked into the dining room.

Danica followed. "Michelle, honey, I do understand your worry, but that's not going to happen."

Michelle turned on her with spiteful eyes. "You don't know that! You can't know that. No one can!"

"That's true, but let's talk about this. Your mom is still in the picture. She might—"

"Right, my mother? Do you even know who you're talking about? She's been in rehab twice. She never sticks around. When she does get clean, it's only long enough to find another nasty, drunk man she can shack up with, and I'm left wondering how long until the next time." Michelle collapsed into a chair. "My life sucks."

"Michelle, your mom is not in rehab anymore. It was your choice not to live with her this time. She worked two jobs before to make ends meet. It's not that she wasn't there for you; she was providing for you. Raising a child alone is hard."

"See, you're on her side," Michelle accused.

"No, I'm not. It's just that I'm sure she's doing the best she can, and maybe you should give her a chance. When was the last time you saw her?" She realized Michelle hadn't mentioned seeing her in months.

"I'm *not* going to see her. I'm the teenager! I'm the one who's supposed to do stupid things, not her!" Michelle stood and crossed her arms, sobbing and huffing in anger.

Danica threw up her hands. "Damn her!" She watched Michelle's eyes grow wide. "How dare she ignore your needs! What the hell is she thinking? Who does she think she is?" She crossed her arms as Michelle dropped hers.

"What are you doing?" Michelle asked in a give-me-a-break voice.

"I'm pissed. She put you in this situation. The hell with disease or addictions that she can't control. Grow up, Mom!"

"You don't believe that."

The anger in Michelle's voice began to dissipate, and Danica pressed on. "I'm serious. To hell with the crutch of addiction. She needs to grow the hell up and take charge of her responsibilities. Your poor grandmother is lying in bed, sick, worrying over her granddaughter and her daughter, and what's your mother doing? Going in and out of some rehab facility, paid for by you know who," she pointed to Nola's bedroom. "Probably loving every God-forsaken minute of that comfortable lifestyle."

"She can't help it. She's addicted."

Inside, Danica silently cheered Michelle on for standing up for her mother, but she said, "Yes, she can! She can stop drinking. She can make a decision to stop working so much when she is sober and to be around more for you."

"You have no idea what you're saying! You're a therapist. You should know addiction isn't a choice!" Michelle seethed.

Good. Let it out. "You said it yourself. A few weeks ago, you said she made those initial choices and she could fix them, remember? What if Nola dies?" She rolled her eyes, pretending to be appalled.

"I was mad. She can't help herself. And Grandma isn't going to die. You're supposed to help me, not freak me out." Michelle stomped back to the living room.

Danica remained in the dining room, arms crossed, hip jutting out like an angry teen. She watched Michelle slowly turn around, a smile creeping across her lips.

"I know what you're doing, you know. I get the whole," she waved her hands up and down at Danica, "pretending-to-be-me thing you're doing."

Danica shrugged, then smiled. "Do you blame me?"

"Yes!" Michelle said, then slumped down onto the couch.

Danica sat beside her and put her arm around her shoulder, pulling her close. "We can't pick our parents, and you do have something to think about. I don't think Nola is going anywhere, but maybe we should go see your mom."

"I don't want to," Michelle admitted.

"Okay, but remember, you're not alone. Your mom is trying, and this time maybe she's found her way to the brighter side. You'll never know unless you give her a chance."

Michelle didn't respond. She just sank into the couch, moving closer to Danica, and to Danica's surprise, she let her arm remain around her. Danica liked the feel of Michelle against her. She remembered sitting in that same position with her own mother, and the comfort it brought was undeniable. She wasn't Michelle's mother, but she was glad she was there for her.

After Michelle calmed down, Danica spent a few private minutes with Nola. She was lying in her bed, fully dressed, with a blanket across just her lap. Her head was propped up on a pillow, and she was reading comfortably.

"How are you feeling?" Danica asked.

"Oh, not great, but not horrible. I have a bad cold, and it's sort of drained me. I'm fine, really, just very tired. I heard it all, and I feel for her. All that mommy drama can turn any girl inside out."

Danica partially closed the door behind her. "How is her mom?"

"It's tough to say. She seems to really be on the straight and narrow now, but, you know."

"But you've seen her?" Danica took in the doilies on the dresser and the heavy cardigan thrown over a rocking chair in the corner. Did every grandmother own a rocker? The meticulously kept bedroom reminded Danica of her grandmother and of how much she missed her.

"Oh, yes. What do you think I do while Michelle is with you?" She set down the book and patted the thin, flowery bedspread.

Danica sat down.

"You know, this comes as no surprise. My husband was an alcoholic. Fifty-two years, until it finally killed him. I hate that Nancy followed in his path."

"It's not really a choi—"

"I've heard it all, and I get it. It's in the genes or some such thing. I don't really understand it, but I hate it just the same." She looked toward the window, as if she were watching a memory unfold. "Nancy is a good person. She was such a good girl growing up. She didn't drink or anything until right after Michelle was born. I don't know. Maybe it was too much for her, raising a baby and all. I should have been around for her more." Nola sat up and put her hand on Danica's leg. "We do what we can, right?"

"Nola, you lived two hours from her when Michelle was born, didn't you? Michelle told me about it."

"Yes, she's right. But mommy guilt runs deep. I try to do right by Michelle. She's a good girl at heart. I worry, though, about her drinking like her mother." Nola picked up a glass of water from the nightstand and took a sip.

"I worry, too. She's watching her own life unravel around her. I think if we teach Michelle about the dangers, the likelihood of it happening to her...She's a smart girl. I think she'll figure it out." Danica hoped her words were true.

"Or, she won't." Nola looked at her and shrugged. "One thing I've learned in my life is that we can teach and hope and pray, but in the end, each person controls their own actions."

"Would it be okay if I went to see Nancy?" Danica wasn't sure if she'd go through with it, but she was contemplating whether it might help.

"Of course. Nancy is thrilled that you're in Michelle's life. I think she really wants to turn her life around, but I also think it's a nasty cycle. Michelle's getting older and she disregards her mother, and that sets her mother back. And really, it's Nancy's own fault." She set down the book. "Any advice for an old woman?"

Danica sighed. "I don't know. Keep loving her; keep teaching her." She looked at the picture on the nightstand of Nola, her husband, and Nancy when she was an infant. "Better yet, keep loving them both, and keep teaching them both. Everyone needs familial support." As she said that, she was thinking of Kaylie, not Nancy.

Chapter Nineteen

Blake's legs bounced nervously beneath Sally's kitchen table. The house was thick with the scent of bouquets, which covered the top of every inch of counter space in the kitchen.

Sally set a cup of coffee in front of Blake and sat down across from him. She clasped her hands around her cup and looked into the dark liquid. "Thanks for coming over," she said.

"Sure, whatever you need. I'm happy to help, but I think before you tell me whatever it is you need to tell me, I need to talk to you about Rusty." He'd wrestled with how to tell Sally about Rusty's excursion all night and finally decided that the truth was the only appropriate path and that not telling her could only lead to a tangled web later.

Sally lifted her eyes. "I'm sure that whatever it is, I already know." She looked back down into the steaming coffee.

"Sally, when I took Rusty to basketball practice the other night, he...well, he didn't really go to practice. I know I should have said something, but with all that you're going through—"

"I know," she said in a flat tone.

"You know?"

She looked up with tear-filled eyes. "That's part of what I wanted to talk to you about. Surely you knew about our problems—mine and Dave's?"

Shit. The last thing Blake felt prepared to handle was their marital issues. "I don't get it. As far as I knew, you and Dave were the happiest couple around. He was always carrying on about your family movie nights, Rusty's basketball practice. Hell, getting him to spend any time *away* from you was like climbing Mount Everest."

A tear slipped down Sally's cheek. She shook her head. "Family movie night? We did that once, like date night. Dave was anything but happy, Blake." She looked down again. "Wow. I really thought you knew."

"No," he said thoughtfully. "Why are you telling me all of this?"

"I'm telling you for Rusty. I know he quit basketball; the coach called me two months ago." She swallowed hard. "But that's also about the time that I realized Dave was really having an affair." She wiped a tear. "Before that, I just thought, I don't know, that something was going on, but I didn't really know what."

"I just can't believe that, Sally. I mean, Dave gave me a hard time for slee—dating so many women all the time." *Did he? Or did he only egg me on?* Blake couldn't be sure anymore. "He adored you and Rusty. He said he went to every basketball practice." Blake ran his hand through his hair and let out a long sigh. "I just don't understand this. I feel like I'm being Punk'd or something."

"I wish you were. Dave was really good at covering his tracks. For the first few weeks, he claimed to be leaving work late, going skiing with you at night."

"Me? He and I hadn't gone skiing for ages before...the accident." Blake took a sip of his coffee and lowered his face to his hands, trying to figure out what was going on. Could he have been that blind to Dave's charades? He lifted his head, anger bubbling into pain in his gut. Danica's words came rushing back to him. *This isn't about you. It's about Sally and Rusty.* He remembered Kaylie's advice of empathy. "I'm sorry that you two were having trouble," he said with compassion. "I still don't understand why you're telling me all of this now. I mean, Dave's gone. There's nothing I can do."

She leaned her elbows on the table and then crossed her arms over her chest. Blake watched her open her mouth, then close it again, struggling to find the right words. He had an urge to hold her in his arms and tell her everything would be all right, but how could he do that when everything was not all right?

"This is embarrassing. The whole awful situation is just...humiliating. I never told my family about it. I didn't know how. I was afraid about what it said about me as a wife." Tears streamed freely down her cheeks. "Rusty is falling apart at the seams, and I just don't know what to do."

Blake was still reeling, trying to get his arms around Dave having an affair. "Does Rusty know?" *That would explain his comments.*

"I don't think so. At least, he's never said as much. But being a teenager is hard, and he's acting out in so many ways. When he came home the other night, the night you drove him to his supposed practice, that was the first time he seemed normal in forever. He's so angry all the time, and whatever went on between you two, well, it seemed to help."

"But I caught him. I'm not a parent, and I am really confused by all of this." Blake ran though his memories of his night with Rusty. He had been so gruff with Blake, so *who-gives-a-shit*, that what she said made no sense to him.

"I should have warned you about his practice." She made air quotes when she said the word *practice*. "But I was in no shape to deal with anything, and he needed the outlet. He doesn't know that I know he's off the team, and I just couldn't sit here with his cursing and stomping around." Anger lifted her voice. "It was selfish of me, and

I'm sorry. I just needed a break." With that, her entire body seemed to collapse. She covered her face with her hands, and her shoulders shook with sobs. She looked like a small child trying to hide from big-world problems. And this one was massive.

"Hey, hey," Blake said softly. "I didn't mind. I'm happy to take Rusty to his...friends, or whatever you need. You weren't being selfish. Really, it's fine." He really needed to talk to Danica. She would know what to do.

"It's just..." Her voice hitched. "Rusty needs a man in his life, not a man who's with me, not a replacement for his father, just someone who gets it, you know? Dave didn't have time for him, and it's unfair to ask it of you, but I'm afraid to ask this of anyone else. Just forget it. I should never have said anything."

Blake was so shocked by the entire situation that he didn't know what else to say.

"She was there, you know, the woman he had an affair with. I saw her in the back of the funeral home."

Blake thought of the woman in the church and began putting two and two together.

"I wanted to yell at her for showing up, but I saw her sitting there alone, crying, and all I could think was how Dave had screwed her over, too." She wiped her eyes.

"Sally," Blake began, but then realized he had no idea what to say. Dave was his friend and business partner, even if he was screwing around. What did friends and business partners say in these circumstances?

"Listen, it is what it is, right? I get it, and believe it or not, I still love the man. And the woman, well, how can I really blame her? Maybe she didn't know he was married, or maybe she did. I don't know. She fell in love with him, I'm sure, for all the same reasons I did. It just sucks."

"I feel like such a fool. I should have known, seen something."

"No, you shouldn't have. He was too good at covering up. But none of that really matters anymore. Right now, he's gone and Rusty is left without a man to turn to."

"Have you thought about a therapist? I mean, I'm not really qualified to step in; you know what I mean?"

"You're a man," Sally said lightly. "You've been a teenage boy, and besides, he won't go to a therapist. I've been playing that angle for the last two months."

"Sally, there's stuff about me that you probably don't know." Blake stood and paced, while Sally remained seated, wiping her eyes, gathering her wits about her like she was redefining a shield.

She sat up straighter, tucked one leg under the other, and cleared her throat.

"Dave probably didn't let you in on much of my life, but I'm a...serial dater, I guess you'd say."

"You're a player; anyone who knows you, knows that," she said like she was stating yesterday's news.

"Yeah, okay, you could put it that way." He hesitated. "Everyone knows that? Really?"

"Blake, it's not like you hide it in any way. I've known you for a few years now and you've never said the same woman's name twice, so yeah, it's pretty obvious. But it doesn't really matter. I mean, I'm not looking for someone to teach Rusty about dating and women, just to be there for him to vent to." She sighed. "Like I said, never mind. It's really not something I should have expected you or anyone else to do."

Blake thought about Rusty. Would he do more harm than good spending time with the kid? Could he turn his back on Dave's son? What would Dave want him to do? *Goddamnit, Dave.* He took a long, hard look at Sally and realized the last thing he wanted to do was hurt her in any way. Sally was broken, the woman in the church was broken, and Dave had done the damage. Blake turned his back to Sally, realizing that what he did with women probably caused similar pain. He'd heard it too many times to count—*Why didn't you call me back? You make me feel like a piece of meat. You used me.*

He turned back to Sally. "If you can overlook what I've done in my life and the things I haven't done—like the right thing. Ever. Then yes, I will help you in whatever way you need with Rusty, and I'll do my best not to have him turn out like me."

Chapter Twenty

Danica had stewed all night over Blake's refusal to give Kaylie her night of pleasure. On one hand, she was proud of him for denying himself the exquisite gratification that she was sure her sister was capable of providing. She knew how difficult it must have been for him to not follow through. She'd seen stronger men than him unable to restrain themselves with her sister. On the other hand, he'd been back in a bar again, obviously flirting with disaster. Danica pushed away thoughts of Blake and Kaylie.

"How did you make out at the funeral?" Danica asked Blake, who sat across from her in a dark T-shirt and jeans. They'd had only a few short sessions together, and Danica knew it could take years to change behaviors. Every client had setbacks, and she expected that of them. So why was she monitoring Blake like he was different? *Concentrate, Danica.*

"I wanted to thank you for helping me through that. I did fine, I guess. I mean, I made it through. I sat in a middle row, as you suggested. So much has happened since then that I feel like it was ages ago. In fact, I feel like every time I come here wanting to talk about one thing, I get sidetracked with other issues that seem to be rising up in my life way too frequently."

I'd like to see something rise. Jesus Christ, Danica, focus!

Instead, Danica thought about Kaylie flying through her door Saturday night. She knew she'd been right not to tell Kaylie about Blake being her client, but what she wasn't sure of was if she should have him as a client at all. Their lives seemed to be a bit too intertwined lately. What if Kaylie had slept with him? If she had, would Danica have had to uphold some sort of unwritten sisterly pact of full disclosure? Would she have had to let Blake know she was Kaylie's sister? Danica was not up to answering any of those hypothetical questions. She'd been so conflicted that she'd woken up at three o'clock in the morning with a killer stomachache, and even now, several hours later, she sat across from Blake with her stomach fluttering in ways she wasn't sure could be qualified as typical therapist woes. Maybe she needed to rethink this relationship.

Trying to regroup, she locked her eyes on his and said, "That happens to a lot of people, I think. But we can talk about anything you want." *Stay focused.* "Sometimes it helps to list the things that we need to address. Then we can prioritize and work our way through them."

"Okay." Blake leaned forward, resting his elbows on his knees.

Danica caught a whiff of his musky cologne and sat back in an effort to remain professional.

"Should I write them down, or..."

"No, just tell me and I'll note them." *A good distraction.*

"Okay, well, there's my bar hopping, Dave's affair, and Rusty." He sat back and looked at Danica.

Did she see something other than worry in his eyes, or was it her imagination? Could she be transferring her lustful feelings onto him? She really needed to get a grip. She noted each issue. "Okay, anything else?" Danica wondered if the heat she felt in her cheeks was visible or just in her mind. She looked down at the notebook again.

Blake smiled. "Isn't that enough?"

She smiled at his joke. "It is, yes. Okay, so which of these do you want to tackle first?"

He looked at her thoughtfully, his eyes traveling over her hair to her face. She felt him staring at her mole. *Stop. Please stop.* He lifted his eyes, then said, "I just realized what's different about you lately. You're not dressed all professional. Wait, that didn't come out right."

She had no control over the smile that spread across her lips. *He noticed. What are you, fourteen? Get a grip.* "Oh, this?" She tried to play it off casually, swatting at her scarf and blouse. "My sister picked it out for me. I'm doing a little soul searching of my own lately."

"Well, I mean no disrespect, but you look great in anything you wear. The blue scarf is really great. It sets off your eyes."

Danica looked down, as uncomfortable as she was excited by his remark. She knew better than to let this go too far. She reined in her smile and gave him a stoic nod. If she was going to remain his therapist, then she had to draw a line somewhere.

"I'm sorry. I didn't mean to say anything inappropriate," Blake added.

"I understand. Let's focus on your list, shall we?" She searched his eyes for whatever had been there before and was met with disappointment. She'd metaphorically slapped his wrist, and as a therapist, she was in no position to apologize. *Damn.*

"I guess the first thing I want to talk about is what to do about Rusty, then Dave, then, well, you know." He looked away.

"Okay, Rusty. Last time we spoke, you'd taken him to practice and he'd ditched it, and if my memory serves me correctly, he said some pretty harsh things about his father." Danica loved when she was on top of her game, and shifting the focus to Rusty allowed her to fall back into line. This, she could handle.

"Yes, well, the story thickens. Sally asked me if I'd take Rusty out sometimes, just so he has someone to talk to. She actually suggested every week. I think she needs the break."

"How do you feel about that? Will you feel like a glorified babysitter, or is there more to this?" Danica watched him settle comfortably in the chair, looking less like a confused, frightened tiger.

"No. I think she really wants him to have a guy to talk to. There's more to it, though, and I just feel funny talking about it all." He clenched his fingers around his thighs.

Danica cleared her throat, trying not to notice that the frightened tiger was back—the criminally handsome, frightened tiger. "Only you can decide what you want to share with me." Why did everything she say end up sounding a lot like she was flirting?

He stood and paced, a habit Danica was getting used to. She only hoped this time it didn't end in him blowing up.

"Sally told me some things about Dave that I'm really having trouble with. I know we talked about my wondering if I was a good enough friend, but my inadequacies..." He turned to face Danica and lifted his eyebrows. "Your word, not mine." He smiled. "My inadequacies of friendship are worse than I thought. Dave was having an affair, and I had no idea."

"Ah, I see. And Sally knew this?" *That poor woman.*

"Yes, she knew, and she knew about Rusty not having practice. I didn't ask for details—I don't want to know, really—but I think I should have known Dave was lying to me, don't you?"

"I didn't know him, but my thought is, not necessarily. You knew what he wanted you to know, or you saw what he wanted you to see."

"That sounds like a cop-out. You're letting me off easy." Blake wasn't joking.

"No, I'm being real. Think about it, Blake. When you pick up a woman, do you let her see everything about your life, or only pieces of it?" *How much would you have let Kaylie see?*

"*Pfft.* That's hardly the same thing. We were friends, and most of the women I've...Well, the women weren't friends; they were just hookups." He leaned back again and crossed his arms.

"It doesn't matter. In any interaction—even ours, now, here—we show only what we want to show. Everyone does it. If Dave was fooling around, for whatever reason, he kept that hidden from you, and probably all the prying in the world wouldn't have changed that."

Blake leaned forward again. "If you could have seen how hurt Sally was...It was awful. I'm sure she wonders every day if it was her fault, or what he did with that other woman—the woman who I actually saw at the funeral home." He shook his head.

"I'm sure she's devastated. Trust is everything in a relationship." She waited until he looked up and then reiterated. "In any relationship."

"So, maybe Dave didn't trust me?"

"Or maybe he did, and he knew you might tell him something he didn't want to hear."

"Whatever the reason, it made me realize that I don't want to be that person. I'm not married, and who knows if I ever will get married, but I don't want to be the person doing the hurting. On any level." His eyes softened and he said, "I'm really glad I'm here, because a few weeks ago I would have probably slit my wrists before allowing myself to feel that way. I don't really want to be that guy anymore. I want to be someone who people are proud of."

"That's a great goal to have, Blake, and I'm confident that whatever you see as your inad—as your faults—you can overcome them and turn things around."

"Sally didn't even tell her family. She was too ashamed. I think on some level, Dave must have been ashamed of himself, too. Otherwise, I'm sure he would have said something to me. And not only that, but Sally doesn't really have strong animosity toward the other woman. She almost understands it." He shook his head. "I just don't get it."

"What goes on in a marriage will never be understood outside of the walls around that union. You can't guess the whys or hows of someone else's relationship, or what they're feeling. Some women might feel as though they'd lost their husband, and nothing else matters, while others might blame the mistress."

171

Blake's forehead wrinkled. "But she should hate that woman. She should hate Dave and maybe even hate me for who I am. I don't know. It just seems weird."

"That's not for you to decide. You can feel bad for Sally and Rusty—or not. You can make a choice to help them through their hard time, or not. But whatever your decision, recognize that you may never understand why Dave did what he did or why Sally feels what she feels." She set the notebook down. She softened her tone. "We can only control who we are, Blake. You are doing all the appropriate things. You are working on yourself, so that you—and no one else matters here but you—can take pride in the person you are." Danica thought about how true that statement was. How many people had she counseled who had expected others to make them happy or complete? That had to come from within, and Danica had found that after her clients found a sense of pride in themselves, the happiness had an easier path to follow. Her thoughts turned to Michelle, which led her to think of Nancy. What was she doing to find a sense of pride in her life? How much must it have hurt to be turned away by Michelle? Danica wondered if she should be having the same conversation with Nancy so she didn't spiral back down into the bottle.

"Intellectually, I get that, and I want to help Rusty. I have no idea what I'll do with him, though."

"What does Sally want you to do?"

"Just be there for him, take him out sometimes." Blake glanced at the clock. "We're almost out of time, and I really want to talk about the last thing today, too."

Danica was relieved. She wanted to hear what he had to say about the bar, and she still wasn't sure if she'd mention that Kaylie was her sister. "Are you okay with the whole Rusty thing? We didn't really define what you should do with him."

"Yeah, it helped. I do want to help him, and I'll find something to do with him. How hard can it be?"

"Okay, then let's move on." Danica's pulse sped up as she thought about Kaylie and Blake together.

"The other night, I went to Bar None." He searched her eyes, and Danica did her best to keep them nonjudgmental. "Kaylie was there."

Oh God. It's now or never. "Yes." *Chicken. I should have told him.*

"Well, she and I...we were talking." He looked down, then sheepishly up at Danica. "Flirting, we were flirting." He blushed. "This is really hard for me, talking about this, but it's important. Especially if I'm going to be a good influence on Rusty."

"It's okay. Take your time. I'm glad you're thinking of Rusty. That's nice."

"Okay, well, I was ready to go home with her, and I mean ready." The way he said *ready* made Danica swallow hard. She envisioned him standing with a huge erection. She felt a flush run up her neck and cleared her throat to distract her own thoughts.

"Go on."

"I didn't do it. I didn't go home with her." He searched her eyes again, and this time Danica smiled. "But you probably already knew that."

Danica didn't confirm or deny his statement. "How did that feel?" The term *cold shower* came to mind.

"Good, actually. She's beautiful, but she would have been a one-night stand, and not that I'm looking for a relationship, but I am trying not to be *that* guy anymore. So, well...you know your sister is very attractive."

Ouch. I know it all too well.

"I was really proud of myself."

"Yes, she is." *If I had a dollar for every time I heard that.* "That's a really positive step, Blake. I'm proud of you." Danica blinked away her fear, gathered courage like a blanket around her.

"Why didn't you tell me she was your sister?" he asked.

"There wasn't a need. When we met, you weren't my client. It would have seemed inappropriate for me to bring it up out of the blue, but now, well, I'm glad you know." She watched him process the information.

A smile crept across his lips. "Good thing I came to my senses before taking her home."

"Blake, you can date anyone you'd like. We're therapist and client, and it's none of my business who you spend time with." *Even if the little, green-eyed monster chases me in circles.*

"Of course, right."

They looked at each other, each waiting for the other to break the silence. Danica felt the pulse of their hearts in the space between them. She reached for the notebook, the pen, anything to carry her out of the trance of the energy emanating from Blake's body.

"Okay, well, what would you like to talk about with regard to...all of that?" she asked.

"Just that I'd done it, and it wasn't as difficult as I'd imagined it might be. But it made me realize that maybe I'm a pretty lonely guy after all. I never would have guessed it, but when I went home that night, my condo was too quiet. I don't spend much time at home—well, I never used to—and lately, when I'm there, I find myself thinking of my father and what he must have felt like without my mom for all those years. I think he was lonely, even though he was busy and he had me."

"You know, being alone doesn't have to equate to being lonely, although it's fine if it does. Maybe you should spend time getting to know yourself a little better. You're a skier and a business owner, but what else?" She glanced at the clock. "In fact, let's use this for our next session. I'm going to give you homework."

Blake lifted his right eyebrow.

"Not an essay, just a list. If you could come up with four things that define you, I think it would help us through this."

"Four things." Blake nodded, thinking. "Okay, sure. And, there's just one thing I want to leave you with."

Danica stood, "Yes?"

Blake stood, just inches from her, his chest within touching distance. He looked down at her, and the space between them once again filled with desire. She saw it in his smoldering, dark eyes, felt it coming off him in waves. *I'm losing it.* Danica took a step past him toward the door.

"I'm beginning to wonder if Dave committed suicide." Blake grabbed his coat and followed Danica. He clenched his thick parka within both fists. That hopeful, *help-me* look returned to his eyes.

"That's a heavy one," Danica said quietly. "Work on your list, and let's talk about that next time."

Blake walked out of her office and turned back as she was closing the door. "I almost forgot to tell you. Jeffrey asked me to be in the wedding. Old college buds and all. So, will I see you next weekend at the pre-wedding hurrah?"

College buds? Danica made a mental note to work with him to explore his friendship with Jeffrey. Maybe Blake wasn't as inept at social and emotional situations as he thought he was. Danica had forgotten all about the pre-wedding party, and now he'd be there, too. How would she pull that off? She'd have to remain sober, that was for sure. "Yup."

Chapter Twenty-One

Blake wondered if everyone experienced life-altering crossroads, or if he was the only one who felt swept away with the avalanche of chaos in his life. He stepped onto the sidewalk, the icy air stinging his cheeks. Was he hallucinating, or had there been some sort of underlying romantic current running between him and Danica? He swore he saw want in her eyes. This celibacy routine must be affecting his senses or something. He zipped his coat and headed for his car.

The main road to AcroSki was backed up, so he took the back roads. When he came to the stop sign at the corner of Cemetery Drive and Nauget Street, he turned right instead of left. He didn't think about where he was going. He didn't intentionally head for Dave's grave. It was as if the car had a mind of its own and he was along for the ride.

He parked in the cemetery lot, grabbed a scarf from the backseat, and wrapped it around his neck, covering his nose from the bitter air. He stepped from the car and stood in the wind, staring in the direction of Dave's grave. There were three cars in the parking lot, though Blake saw no other people on the cemetery grounds. He didn't know what he was going to do when he got there, but he was drawn toward Dave's grave. He shouldered the wind, and a few moments later, he was standing above the freshly tilled earth. With his hands buried deep in his coat pockets, he stared at the rich, brown soil, a sharp contrast to the fresh, snowy carpet around the gravesite.

Blake looked up at the sky. "Dave? Was I a good friend? Was it my life that made you reach outside of your marriage, because if it was, buddy, I'm sorry. It's not so great." He heard the footsteps before she appeared beside him. He expected to find Sally, but instead was faced with the woman from the back of the church.

"Hi," she said softly.

"Hello," Blake said, and shot his eyes back to the ground, feeling awkward in her presence. What if Sally came by and saw them? Would she think he'd been lying and that he'd known about her the whole time?

"Dave was a good man," she said.

Blake nodded, unsure how good of a man Dave had really been. "Were you a friend?" Blake couldn't help it. He wanted to know if she'd cover up the affair.

She faced him, her wavy, blond hair tucked beneath a red, knit hat. Her brown eyes were painfully small. She wore red lipstick that matched the bright shade of her hat, and her long, gray, fitted coat hung almost to her knees. She looked like one of those little porcelain dolls that had their makeup painted on. She crossed her hands over her chest, warding off the wind. "Yes. You're Blake, right?"

Surprised, he said, "Mm-hmm. Do I know you?"

She turned away again. "No, I suppose you wouldn't." She thrust her hands in her pockets.

Blake glanced at her out of the corner of his eye. She was a petite woman, no taller than his chest. "How did you know Dave?" he asked.

She kicked her rubber boot at a mound of wayward dirt. "We helped each other with things."

"Things?" He was digging himself deeper into a hole he wasn't sure he wanted to be in, but he needed to understand what went on between them, and why Dave would ruin his family for this woman.

"I knew Dave when we were teenagers, and we hadn't seen each other for years, until I moved back here. Back home. We were...friends."

Blake felt the heat of anger despite the brisk air. He turned and faced her. "Friends?" *You're not getting off that easy*. "How is it that you know who I am, but I have no idea who you are?"

"You're Dave's business partner," she said, making no effort to avoid his confrontational gaze. "Dave told me all about you." She looked up at the sky, as if searching for an answer. "Dave and I were...he was...I have a seventeen-year-old son." She looked into Blake's eyes, and he saw the answer.

"Dave's son?" Blake felt as if he'd been kicked in the gut. *Sally. Rusty. Oh God.*

She nodded. Her hair fell into her eyes and she left it there. She spoke softly, her words trembling in the cold. "We were so young. He didn't know about Chase. He was trying to do the right thing, getting to know him, spending time with him."

"Sleeping with you," Blake accused.

"No." She shook her head. "No, it wasn't like that. He was just trying to figure out what to do, how to tell his wife." She wiped her eyes with her gloved fingertips. "He loved her, and while he was spending time with Chase, he wasn't going to leave her for me; it wasn't like that."

"But Sally knows about you two. She said she—"

She shook her head, revealing her honest eyes. "He tried to tell her about Chase, and she assumed there was more to it."

"But he let her believe it. She's heartbroken and falling apart more with each day because she thinks he was having an affair."

"He was, sort of, but not with me. Emotionally, I guess he was...dividing his time. He was spending time getting to know Chase. He wanted to wait until they were on solid ground before bringing Sally and Rusty to meet him. There was a lot to deal with."

"Why now? Why did you come back after so many years?" Blake's rage mounted. "You needed money, wanted a husband?"

"No," she said adamantly. "I came back because my father died and I needed to take care of his affairs. I saw Dave at the store, and we started talking. He did the math. I never even brought it up. It wasn't my plan for him and Chase to meet—ever. It just happened."

Blake turned around and pulled his shoulders up against the wind, then turned back to her, spewing his anger without restraint. "Do you understand what his wife is going through? He must have spent loads of time with you—or with Chase—at his family's expense, and now they're left believing he didn't love them."

"He was trying to do the right thing." Tears fell from her eyes.

"Yeah, well, he's dead, and a lot of people are hurting. What now?" Blake had to get to Sally; he had to explain what was going on. Would she even care? Dave had stolen their family time and they'd never get that back.

"I don't know, okay? I have my own son to worry about. He only just got to know his father, and now he's gone."

Blake had enough of his own shit to deal with. The last thing he needed was someone else's mess on his plate. Now, more than ever, he wondered if Dave had purposely missed the angle of the jump, sending himself tumbling to his death. As he walked back to his car, he mulled over the possibilities and wondered if Dave had felt pulled too far under the weight of his own life's complexities to ever find his way out again. Blake couldn't imagine that the love Dave showed toward Sally had been feigned. Maybe the possibility of losing her was just too much for him to take.

He unlocked his car, wondering if the woman had been telling the truth, or if Dave had been having an affair with her. Then he realized that it didn't really matter. What he'd given her was his time and emotional energy—the thing that Sally and Rusty had needed most.

He stopped at a red light on the way to his shop. There he was, at the corner of the street that ran straight to his shop and the one that led in the direction of Sally's house. When the light changed, he continued on toward AcroSki.

Chapter Twenty-Two

Danica sat in Nancy's apartment, watching her move nervously from the living room to the kitchen, returning with a plate of cheese and crackers and a pitcher of ice water. There was little furniture in the living room—a worn, green couch with a dark blue throw across the back cushions, a coffee table, and a scratched, wooden shelving unit that looked like it had seen better days. Gracing each shelf were photographs of Michelle, from infancy to her current school picture, which Danica recognized as the same photograph that Nola had framed and placed on her piano. There were no stacks of clutter, no bills piling up that she could see. The apartment was small and tidy, with the kitchen just off of the living room. Danica peered in and took note of the cleanliness, dishes drying neatly on a rubber drying rack. It was easy for Danica to envision Nancy curled up on the couch with a cup of black tea, wondering what her daughter was doing at that moment.

"I'm sorry that I don't have something more to offer you, but you know, no sugar and all that. Something about sugar increasing the desire for alcohol."

Danica had seen pictures of Nancy, but she hadn't realized how much Michelle looked like her until she was sitting beside her. They had the same oval chin, the same slender fingers, and the same nervous way of hiding behind their hair. "This is just fine." Danica reached for a glass and filled it with ice water.

Nancy couldn't have been much older than her mid-thirties, but worry had etched deep lines across her forehead. "I really appreciate all you're doing for Michelle," she said sheepishly.

"Michelle is a really good kid. You should be proud of her."

"Oh, I am proud of her. I'm more proud of her than I've ever been of anyone in my life. My mother, too. To pick up the pieces like she does. I know it's not easy for either of them."

You've got that right. "That's kind of why I'm here. I know it's none of my business, but how are you doing with your recovery?"

"You have every right to ask," she said. "I've got myself a job waitressing at the Friday's in town. I don't serve alcohol. I go to all of my meetings, and this time I haven't felt the desire to go back to drinking. Not once." She looked up with a tentative smile.

"That's great, Nancy. I'm sure it's been a very difficult time for you." Danica realized that no matter what Nancy told her, she couldn't know what to believe. Recovery wasn't a clearly defined path, and rebound was likely for most recovering alcoholics. No matter how much Nancy wanted to change, there was always the quiet presence of the addiction on her shoulders. No wonder Michelle was reluctant to let her mother back into her life. She could lose her mother again at any moment.

"It is. Don't get me wrong." She sat back against the couch cushions and blinked several times, as if she were trying to hold back tears. "Michelle is everything to me. I got lost for a while there, running with the wrong crowd, feeling put upon for having to care for a child alone. I don't know." She crossed her legs. "I don't mean to rationalize any of what I've done. It was all a way to hide, I guess. In a way, I was running away from my responsibilities, I suppose. But this time, things were different. I wasn't sitting there feeling put upon or angry at the world for whatever I used to feel. This time, all I could think about was how lucky I am to have Michelle and how much I've let her down. She sees me for what I was, for what I am, and I'm dead set on fixing that. There's no going back for me. I'll never make her feel that way again, if I can help it."

"Are you getting help beyond the support groups?" Danica knew from Nola that she was attending weekly support meetings.

Nancy nodded vehemently. "Oh, yes. I see a counselor, Dr. Paltron, every week, and I've even asked her to give me random urine tests." She scribbled a phone number on a piece of paper and handed it to Danica. "Call Dr. Paltron, please. She can tell you how I'm doing. I have nothing to hide."

Danica took the paper. "You asked her to test you?"

"Yes. I don't want to slip back into that life, and with that hanging over my head, well, it's a reminder."

Danica was impressed. In her experience, addicts were always on the edge of falling back into the throes of their addiction. Nancy's case was slightly different. She hadn't spent her whole life moving in and out of rehab. She'd had a hard time dealing with the death of Michelle's father, a drug addict who had never been a part of Michelle's life, but whom she had remained desperately in love with.

"I know what you're thinking," Nancy said. "What about when that's not enough, the threat of a urine test? But the truth is, I know in my heart that this is it. I'm not going back to that life. I'm ashamed of the pain I've caused Michelle." A tear slipped down her cheek. "I will make this work. I will not allow myself to screw up again. That girl needs me, faults and all. She needs her mother."

"Well, everyone needs their parents, but Michelle is in a really stressful period in her life. Being a teenager is not an easy time for anyone."

"I know. This whole mess was wrapped around her father dying. Michelle didn't know him, but I loved him. I was sucked into his life once—the first time I went into rehab—but I was not going to be sucked in again. I didn't realize that his death could push me over the edge. It was my fault. I let myself hide in the fog of alcohol, in a place where I should have been too numb to feel. But I wasn't too numb to feel. I was hurt and lonely, and now I'm ashamed." She moved to the edge of the couch. "I still felt the pain of his loss. I couldn't hide from it. Now I've accepted it and I'm able to move forward." She must have seen something in Danica's eyes, because she added, "Michelle is everything to me. I *will* move forward. I will make that girl proud, if it's the last thing I do."

Danica had heard the same thing before from her clients. Some meant it; some didn't. She believed, from the pitch of Nancy's voice and the desperation and confidence intertwined in her eyes, that she meant it—at least at that very moment. But it was Michelle she was worried about. "It's not me you have to convince. Michelle's not sure what she can trust. She's seen you at your worst, so it may take her some time to trust you again."

Nancy nodded, wiped her tears with her sleeve. "I know that, and I'll wait as long as it takes." Nancy lifted her eyes to Danica's. "From what my mother has told me, you're really helping Michelle deal with things. Can you tell me how she's doing? Is she into anything...bad? Have I screwed her up in that way?"

Danica thought of Michelle in the museum, thoughtfully looking over the artwork, and the way she came into her own in the Village. "I think she's doing just fine, but she's struggling with her relationship with you and whether she'll ever live the life of a typical mother and daughter."

"Well, we're anything but typical," Nancy admitted.

An alarm sounded in another room. "I'm sorry," she said, walking toward the offending noise. "I have to get ready for work." She came back from the bedroom with an envelope in her hand. "Would you mind giving this to Michelle?"

"Um..." Danica worried what the envelope might contain. Last wishes? Hopes for the future? She looked at the envelope without reaching for it.

Nancy shrugged. "It's just, she won't talk to me, and I miss her so much, so I started writing her letters. Then I realized that a teenage girl probably doesn't want a string of sappy letters, so I wrote just this one, told her how I felt, that I'm sorry, and, well, some other stuff I thought she needed to know. I want her to know I'm doing everything I can and I will remain sober. She needs to know this."

Danica felt a rush of relief. "Sure, I'll give it to her next week." She took the envelope.

Danica left Nancy's apartment and headed for her office. She checked her watch, and knowing she had no more clients that afternoon, she picked up her cell phone and dialed Kaylie's number.

"To what do I owe this pleasure?" Kaylie joked.

"Do you have a dress for the party this weekend? Because I don't." She listened to Kaylie squeal with excitement on the other end of the phone line. "I'm thinking that I need something that's more like the new me, less..."

"Frigid?" Kaylie offered.

"I wouldn't go that far, but something like that. Meet me in the Village?"

"I only have an hour. I'm singing tonight at the Mantra." The Mantra was the restaurant that kept Kaylie's bills paid. Danica had seen her sing only three times. Watching the old men eye her younger sister always turned her stomach.

"Great, I'll take it. Meet me at the center lot."

They looked through racks of eclectic dresses and skirts. Kaylie, looking twenty-two in her UGGs and tight jeans, and Danica feeling thirty-nine, instead of twenty-nine, in her professional work attire. Why did she do this to herself? She'd have to find a heavy, unattractive friend to go out with so she felt better about herself. *Oh God. Now I sound like one of my clients.*

"Dr. Snow!"

Danica spun around at the sound of Belinda Trenton's voice.

"Weird seeing you here, outside of your office," Belinda gushed. "Shopping?" She eyed Kaylie.

"I'm working on her wardrobe," Kaylie said.

It wasn't often that Danica's clients came in contact with her outside of her office, but this was the second client who had come across Kaylie in as many weeks, and Danica felt it like a noose tightening around her neck. She'd never realized Allure was such a small town. She preferred to keep clients and family separate. "Just checking out a few things." Danica smiled in a tight-lipped fashion, hoping she portrayed a professional courtesy instead of a friendship.

"What do you think of this?" Belinda asked, waving to her own clothing.

How had Danica missed her black flats and flare-bottom jeans. They were a big improvement over the painted-on skinny jeans and heels. "That look suits you well," Danica said, beaming with a modicum of pride. Maybe she was helping after all.

"See, I listen to the things you say."

Belinda examined Kaylie up and down with a look of jealousy—didn't they all? "Love your outfit," she said.

Kaylie smiled in the uncomfortable way that said, *There must be a reason you're seeing my sister, so I don't want to associate with you.*

"Well, I'll leave you two to have fun. See you next week!"

Belinda left the store, and Danica breathed freely again.

Kaylie touched her arm and whispered, "Now that the crazy girl is gone, how about this?" She held up a brown, suede, thigh-length dress complete with fringe at the bottom.

"Don't call her that, and what am I? An Indian princess?" Danica watched Kaylie shove the dress back on the rack and began going through the clothes with a scrutinizing eye.

"Sor-ry. I'm just trying to spice things up a bit."

Maybe this was a mistake. "How's Chaz?"

"He treats me like a queen. He calls, he e-mails. He sends flowers."

She recognized Kaylie's bored tone. "Sounds perfect."

Kaylie sighed. "I guess, if you like that stuff." She pulled a simple, black dress from the rack. It crossed in the front and tied at the hip—a good look for Danica. The trim was done in a gold, sparkly threading, adding just a touch of something interesting.

"Me? I'd love that stuff. It sounds like he really likes you." Danica took the dress from her sister's hand and headed for the dressing room with Kaylie on her heels.

"He does."

"But?" Danica slipped into the dressing room while Kaylie waited outside the curtain.

"I don't know. I really like him, but everything is too easy. I feel like things will just fall apart and I won't know they're going to."

Danica peeked out of the curtain. "You're afraid of being Mom. You think that just because Dad blindsided Mom with an affair, Chaz will do that to you?" She closed the curtain.

"Maybe. I don't know."

Behind the curtain, Danica slipped the dress on and tied it at her waist. She looked fantastic, and she wondered if she'd lost weight. She never paid enough attention to know if she went up or down a few pounds until things settled like an old house and she needed new clothes. "Well, you're not Mom, and easy is good, Kaylie."

She came through the curtain and Kaylie gasped. "Dan, oh my God. You look so beautiful!"

Danica spun around, feeling young and pretty. She wanted to flounce around the room and enjoy the feeling. "Do you think so?"

"I know so." Kaylie hugged Danica. "Whatever has come over you lately, it suits you well."

Danica felt her cheeks flush. "Kaylie, listen, whatever happened between Mom and Dad was their own shit. You aren't Mom; Chaz isn't Dad. Just allow yourself to be happy for once. Don't sabotage it." She disappeared behind the curtain again, admiring herself in the mirror before slipping back into her own clothes.

As she paid for the dress, Kaylie leaned on the counter, her chin resting on her palm.

"What?" Danica asked.

"How does it feel to be you?" She stood. "I mean, you've got your shit together. You know what to do in a relationship—even if you don't have one—and you're not afraid of anything." She sighed. "It must be...nice."

"If only you knew, Kaylie." She wanted to admit her insecurities to Kaylie, but it felt too good to be looked up to. She smiled, put her arm around her sister, and they headed for their cars.

The next few days flew by with a flurry of client meetings, leaving Danica in a state of emotional fatigue by nine o'clock each night. She'd made the time to call Nancy's counselor, who confirmed that not only was she doing well, but that she'd been a stellar client while at rehab. Dr. Paltron had said she thought that the weekly urine tests were overkill. Nancy was among the few adults who she had high hopes for. She was not a typical rehab patient. According to Dr. Paltron, Nancy had been on a drinking binge one afternoon and Michelle found her. Michelle's father had just died, and she and Michelle got into a fight. Nola got involved, and Nancy committed herself to rehab. Dr. Paltron admitted that she thought it was almost an overreaction for Nancy to have been in rehab, but she understood the concern on Nancy's part, given her father's substance-abuse history; she left Danica feeling far more confident than before she'd made the phone call. She'd been under the impression that Nancy had been a drinker for months. The way Michelle told the story, Nancy was always drinking. Danica was beginning to see even more clearly how a teen's perspective could skew a situation even when they weren't doing so on purpose. And she felt bad for Michelle, whose own hurt over the situation had probably caused her to embellish her mother's situation.

The night of Jeffrey and Camille's party arrived with an unusual warmth to the normally frigid nighttime air. Danica was not looking forward to the evening. She'd much rather be curled up in her favorite sweatpants in front of the television, or deep into the story of a good book, than be worrying about how Kaylie and Blake might react when they saw each other again—but she'd never let down Camille like that.

She arrived in her new black dress and a pair of her comfortable Nine West heels. She wasn't about to twist her ankle again and make a fool out of herself. She walked into the restaurant, and as she neared the private back room, butterflies let loose in her stomach. She peered into the room, looking, she realized, for Blake.

A large hand embraced her shoulder. A whisper landed in her ear. "Spying or going in?"

Her pulse raced. *Blake.* The ridiculous desire to turn and kiss him crossed her mind. She pushed it away and took a deep breath. "Going in," she said without turning back to look at him. She took a step forward, secretly hoping his hand wouldn't drop from her shoulder. It did. She feigned a smile and crossed the well-appointed dining room to where the other bridesmaids had gathered.

"Danica!" Camille squealed. The other girls gave her a group hug and someone handed her a Manhattan. "Tonight we're pretending we're in New York, so Manhattans all night long."

Who was she to deny their fun? She took a sip, relishing in the sweet taste of vermouth and cherry. She reminded herself to go easy and watched Blake out of the corner of her eye. He stood with Jeffrey and the other groomsmen, laughing, with his head tossed back and looking delicious in his gray slacks and black sweater. He looked over just as she realized she was staring. He lifted his glass in her direction. *Damn.* She turned away and gulped down her drink, motioning to the bartender for another.

Danica scanned the room for Kaylie, who was mysteriously missing. "Have you seen my sister?" she asked Marie.

"I know she's coming. She called me earlier." Marie looked around. "She's probably out with Chaz. I swear that man is so in love with her."

"That means he won't be around for long," Camille mused.

"Yeah." Marie drew her eyebrows together. "What's up with that?"

"You know Kaylie. She just likes to have fun." Danica didn't want to go into any family drama with Marie—or anyone else for that matter.

"Well, I think she likes him just as much. I mean, she's always with him."

"She is?" *Why didn't I know that?*

"She's always at his place, or he's at hers. If I didn't know Kaylie so well, I'd almost think she's smitten with him."

Danica wondered what all of Kaylie's earlier drama had really been about. Could her sister just want her attention, or was she really worried that she'd be like their mother?

"Mr. Hottie is heading for you. I'll disappear." Marie winked.

The room grew smaller as Blake approached. *Get it together. He's a client.*

"You look ravishing," he said, then added, "I mean that in the most professional way, of course."

Why do you have to be so cute? "Of course. Thank you." She felt herself blush and silently cursed. Danica watched the waiters bringing salads to the enormous round table set up in the middle of the room. The others were already claiming their chairs, and Danica's heart raced as she realized that there were only three open seats, two beside each other and one between Marie and Stephanie. "We should sit," she said, feeling uneasy beside him.

He placed his hand—his warm, sensuous palm—against her lower back and led her to one of the two seats that were side by side. The heat of his palm drew all of her attention. She recognized a possessive move when she saw, or rather, felt it, but she was too drawn in to move away. He pulled out a chair for her and she sat, trying to ignore Marie's eager smile of approval.

Danica found her voice and pushed it past the nerves that tickled her throat. "Has anyone heard from Kaylie?" She didn't dare look at Blake. She felt the heat of him sitting next to her, and that was difficult enough. She didn't need to fall into his gorgeous eyes or smell the alcohol on his breath. Why was that smell so seductive, anyway?

"She texted. She'll be here soon," Camille answered.

Danica listened to the men talk about "the old ball and chain" and the women talk about dresses, flowers, and the impending honeymoon. She couldn't help but notice that Blake was silent beside her. She stole a glance in his direction and noticed the tight lines around his eyes and the clenching muscles in the side of his jaw. She fought the urge to touch his cheek and tell him everything would be okay.

He turned to her and feigned a smile. Whether it was her therapist brain or her womanly empathy, she couldn't be sure, but she asked in a whisper, "Are you all right?"

Blake nodded and set his napkin on the table. "It's Dave and that woman. I'm just having a hard time with it all."

Danica leaned in closer to him. "See, you are a good friend. If you weren't, you wouldn't give it a thought."

"I met her the other day at the cemetery when I was...I don't even know what I was doing there." Blake looked at her with pain in his eyes. He leaned in closer, until his mouth was beside her ear. His breath was hot on her neck, sending goose bumps down her chest. "They had a child together seventeen years ago, and she said they weren't having an affair, but he was getting to know his kid."

Danica tried her hardest to concentrate on the words he spoke, but the feel of his breath was too distracting. She felt a pull down low in her belly, and she felt her hand reaching for his leg as he leaned toward her. She pulled her hand back and leaned away from him. *What the hell am I doing?* She didn't think about what she must look like until she heard Blake's next question.

"I'm sorry. Should I not have said that here?"

Shit. "What? No, that's fine." Said what? she wondered. *Damn it, Danica. Pull yourself together.*

"We can talk another time. I'm sorry," he said, and turned back toward the table.

"I'm so sorry I'm late!" Kaylie's enthusiasm sent renewed energy around the room.

Thank God.

"We went for a drive this afternoon and got held up." Kaylie leaned down and kissed Camille's cheek. "I'm so sorry, Camille. You know I would never be late on purpose."

Danica watched Blake for signs of attraction toward Kaylie, but his eyes were heavy as he focused on his plate. She'd made him feel like he'd done something wrong again. What was wrong with her? She couldn't deal with that right then. She had to get through the evening and get the hell out of there. It was obvious to her that she could deal with Blake only in the office, not outside of it. "I'm sorry," she whispered to Blake. "We can talk about this Monday." She turned her attention to the discussion Kaylie and Camille were having about the wedding. Kaylie was asking if it would be all right if she brought a date.

"A date?" Camille asked. "But when we made the invitations, you said you would never bring a date—"

"Because it was too limiting," Marie, Stephanie, and Laurie all chimed in together.

"Yeah, well." She looked up at Danica. "Things change, I guess. Would it be okay?"

"Of course, Kaylie. What's one more person?" Camille squeezed Kaylie's hand.

Danica didn't have the mental ability to weed through her sister's ever-changing feelings about the men in her life any more than she was able to deal with sitting next to Blake with his knee less than an inch from hers, his cologne wafting into her space like a hook reeling her in, and those lonely, confused eyes calling out to the therapist in her. Her head swooned with lascivious thoughts, and her desire was out of control, like she might lean over and kiss him at any moment. She didn't trust herself.

She looked down and focused on the meal before her. She could pick up a fork and find her mouth. She could pick up a drink and suck it down. Baby steps, she told herself. Danica focused on the clanking of forks to plates, the discussions about the toast of the best man, and she tried her hardest to pay attention to the bits and pieces of Kaylie's conversation with Marie, but her head was full of conflict and her heart was full of lust for Blake.

Finally, the meal ended and she saw an escape. Danica stood from the table. "I have an early day tomorrow, so I'm afraid I'm going to bow out early tonight." She managed her most sincere smile. "Camille, Jeffrey, thank you. I'm really excited about your wedding. It's going to be amazing."

She hurried from the restaurant and into the safety of her car. Danica banged her head on the steering wheel and let her head rest there while she asked herself why she was acting like such an idiot.

A knock on the window startled her.

Blake was peering through the window. She took a deep breath and rolled it down. The cold air whipped through the car. "Mr. Carter," she said in her most professional voice.

"Danica, can we talk?"

"Sure, Monday." She looked straight ahead, not at Blake.

"I'm sorry. I didn't mean to bring your work into this and ruin your night. I just needed to talk." Honesty and worry laced his every word.

"It's all right. It's not that."

"It wasn't? What did I do? What did I say?"

She stole a look at him, and if she could feel a heart tear into shreds, hers was doing it right then. His face was stricken with confusion. Danica opened the door and stepped from the car. She didn't know if it was a good idea or not, but it was as if her legs had a mind of their own, and they were headed toward the side of the restaurant. He followed beside her.

Stars illuminated the clear sky like hundreds of tiny beacons of light. They walked along the side of the building to an outside dining area that was used only in the summer and offered a spectacular view of the snowy mountaintops.

"Blake, I'm not sure we should—"

He stepped in front of her, cutting off her words, and looked down at her with an intense gaze. "Please, don't push me away. You've done more for me in the past few weeks than anyone has done for me ever. In my whole life."

The thin, gray line she desperately wanted to cross held more than just right or wrong. Her career hung in the balance. Danica felt her body being drawn closer to him. *God help me.* The heat that emanated between them had a pulse of its own. She knew in that moment that she was done being his therapist—maybe even being a therapist altogether.

He put his hands on her arms, and she tried again to disconnect from the warmth beneath them.

"I don't mean to keep screwing things up. I know there's a client-therapist relationship, and I don't mean to cross any lines."

She looked down at his hands on her arms, her breasts moving up and down with each heavy breath. Her voice failed her. Had she misinterpreted his actions?

"You set me straight," he said. "You listened; you helped me; you didn't just fawn over me. I need that."

Great. I'm a good therapist. Danica pushed her shoulders back, and his hands dropped to his sides. "That's what I'm here for," she said. Her hands felt heavy, like they didn't belong hanging by her sides. She longed to lift them, touch his hips, place her fingertips on his lower back and pull him in close.

"I can't talk to anyone the way I talk to you," he admitted.

"It's part of the charm of being a therapist," she said. It was common for clients to be attracted to their therapists, she told herself, but not common, or acceptable, for it to be the other way around. *Damn it.* Had she jumped the gun? Was it foolish to think about giving up her career? Maybe he didn't want her in *that* way after all.

"I used to be able to ignore all the bad stuff around me, but now, now I process it in a way I never thought I would, or even could. The strange thing is that everything I'm processing, I realize they're things that I never want to do. I'm done hurting people. And what's even stranger is that when it happens, when I'm in the midst of these...revelations...all I want to do is pick up the phone and call you."

Oh God. Was it possible for her legs to stop working? She resumed walking down a paved path through the trees just to be sure she wouldn't melt right there and then. Moonlight sparkled above them, illuminating the Christmas lights that the restaurant kept in the trees year-round. If she weren't so conflicted, Danica might think she was having the most romantic night of her life. Instead, she had to be careful how she responded to his admission. She stopped walking and faced him head on. She'd always believed in honesty, and it had served her well. Under the light of the moon, speaking to the only man to make her stomach flutter in months, if not years, she took the path of honesty once again.

"I don't think we should do this anymore," she said. There. She said it. Her stomach hurt, her heart ached, and she held her breath, waiting for his response.

"Walk?" he joked.

Despite her nerves, she laughed.

"I need you, Danica," he said.

But not in the same way I'm needing you lately.

"I don't think I can sort through all of this without you." He lifted his hand to touch her cheek, and she watched his face change as he caught himself and dropped it to his side instead. "I'm sorry if I screwed this up," he said honestly.

How long could she play this game? Did she seriously misread him? Did he want her to just be his therapist? The words flew from her mouth before she could stop them. "Damn it, Blake. Is it just me, or is there something more here? I feel like a high school girl crushing on the football player, and yet there you are, telling me that you need me as your therapist, but your body language—"

He touched her cheek, giving away nothing with his serious eyes.

Shit. "Well, okay," she said. *Damn it.* Tears welled in her eyes. She was such a fool. Why didn't she leave well enough alone? She turned to leave, and Blake caught her by the arm.

"You mean, you *like* me, like me?" he asked.

She didn't answer.

"You like me. You *like* me?" A grin spread across his beautiful lips.

"Okay, enough. I'll refer you to a new therapist." *And find a new career.* "I'm sorry for my unprofessionalism."

In the next breath, he drew her body against his own and wrapped her in the warmth of his arms. His lips pressed against hers, the sensual, intoxicating smell of him penetrating her senses, and she relaxed into his embrace. His tongue explored her mouth with sensuality, not rushing or taking her, but savoring her, tasting her. His hands spread across her back, and she was lost in his kiss, and the smell of his cologne, and the night air across her warm cheeks. She felt lighter than air, as if she were floating away on a cloud. His lips softened, and he placed gentle kisses on her pulsating lips.

"I thought it was just me," he admitted.

Danica's trembling hands were rooted to his back, her eyes glued to his. She ached to kiss him again, but the therapist in her knew better. Even if she was going to throw away her career, she still knew right from wrong. "We can't do this. It's wrong. You're my client—or were my client—or whatever." *Oh God. Help me.*

"I am your client."

"I can't have a relationship with my client. It's unethical." She was powerless to pull herself from his arms.

"I need you as my therapist." He kissed her again. "I want you as my girlfriend."

Danica pulled away. "I could lose my license. I can't do this." *I want to do this.* She'd been so careful about who she dated and how she handled herself in her professional and personal life. She should know better than to throw that away for a man who was in only the beginning stages of his therapy. But she could not deny the desire that stretched from her fingertips to her toes and burrowed into every nook and cranny in between. *Crap.* Her legs carried her in the direction of the parking lot.

"Danica, wait." He came after her, falling in step beside her. "I do need your help with my personal life, getting on track, understanding things."

"I can't help you with that now." She stopped walking and turned toward him, her voice angrier than she'd thought it would be. "We kissed, Blake. We can't kiss. I can't be your therapist now that we've kissed. It's not right."

The silence between them was broken only by the night breeze through the trees. For the first time in her life, Danica didn't have an answer. She stormed away, a mountainous lump pushing against her throat. By the time she reached her car, tears streaked her cheeks like rain.

Chapter Twenty-Three

Sunday morning found Danica puffy-eyed and listless. She'd spent the night angry at herself, sexually frustrated, and worst of all, she knew she'd let down a client—a very hot client who also needed her help.

She went through her morning routine like an automaton, showering, dressing in her pre-finding-herself boring attire of black slacks and a gray, cashmere sweater. She gave up on her wild hair and left the house with what her mother might have called her sixties' Afro look. She didn't give a damn. She'd lived her life carefully, always putting work and professionalism before her own needs, and she'd been proud of who she was. She'd thrown that all away in one night—over one goddamned kiss. Any way she looked at it, she was an idiot. Now her client was left to fend for himself—no, she'd find him another therapist. More importantly, she couldn't help but wonder if she had walked away from the one man whom she might actually have been falling for. Thoughts of the way he'd jumped into changing his behavior, mostly on his own accord, flitted through her mind. His serious and sad eyes when he spoke of how he didn't want to hurt anyone anymore bored into her. If she were truthful with herself and remembered the way he'd eyed the blonde, she'd tell herself what she might tell Kaylie about a guy like him: *Get over him. Once a player, always a player.* Despite knowing what was best, and what was dangerous, Danica still couldn't stop thinking about him. Thank God she had Michelle to distract her today.

Danica was glad to see Nola back on her feet, pink-cheeked and bright-eyed, when she picked up Michelle. Michelle was dressed in her typical black attire, but when they stepped from the car and headed toward the bakery, Michelle pulled the multicolored scarf from her purse and wrapped it around her neck.

"I love that look on you," Danica said.

"I feel funny wearing it around the kids at school, but I do love it. Thank you," Michelle said.

They sat at their usual table by the window. Michelle ate her croissant and watched Danica pick at hers.

"Are you okay today?" Michelle asked.

Danica tried to smile, but felt her cheeks fall flat. "Yeah, just a little tired." She was the Big Sister. Danica knew she'd better pull her act together, for Michelle's sake.

A group of four teens burst through the door. Michelle cast a quick look at them, then cowered into her chair, expertly shaking her head so her hair fell over her cheek—a ready-made veil.

Danica took note of the effervescent teens, laughing and joking in the way kids did at that age—too loud and ignorant to notice or care about the stares of others. She watched Michelle take another quick glance at them. When they'd first begun going out for breakfast, Michelle had picked that particular bakery because she said no one from her school would go there. Now she sat with her shoulders hunched, tugging at one end of her scarf, slowly unwrapping it from around her neck. It was clasped between her hands when the tallest boy came and stood beside the table. His hair flopped trendily over his eyes, the rest at a shaggy-chic, ear level.

"I know you," he said, not in an unkind way.

Danica watched silently, feeling the pain of Michelle's embarrassment.

"Hey," Michelle said without looking up.

"What's up?" he said to Michelle, then turned toward Danica. "Hey, I'm Brad." He waved, then put his hands in his sweatshirt pockets.

"Hi, Brad. I'm Danica, Michelle's...friend."

The boy stood there, a friendly smile plastered on his face. He looked from Michelle to his friends, then back at Michelle again.

Danica wanted to say something to break the awkward silence, but she knew teens too well. The wrong thing could set them off.

"Great scarf," he said.

Michelle smiled beneath her hair.

"Come on, B-man," another boy hollered.

"Hey, we're heading to the Village. Wanna go?" He looked at Michelle with the same friendly smile that had been there since he'd arrived at the table.

Look up, Michelle. Look up.

"Thanks, but we're kinda busy," she said, still looking at the scarf in her lap.

"Michelle, I don't—"

A harsh stare stopped Danica in her tracks. "Um, yeah, we kind of have plans, sorry," Danica said to Brad, whose smile quickly faded. He shot a look from Michelle to his friends and back again.

"Okay, well, maybe another time then." He walked backward toward the door, where his friends were waiting.

"Who was that?" one girl asked.

"Girl from school. She's cool," he said on their way out the door.

Danica's heart slammed against her chest with excitement. Brad liked Michelle. He'd called her cool. Surely Michelle would be happy.

Michelle didn't move from her cocoon.

"He seemed nice," Danica said.

Michelle shrugged.

"Is there something about him that I'm not seeing?"

Michelle shook her head. "Can we get out of here? Please?"

Boy, did Danica know that feeling. She gathered their breakfasts and headed for the door with Michelle in tow, eyes locked on the floor, scarf clenched within her hands.

They walked in silence toward the art gallery, where Michelle had said she wanted to go after breakfast. Brad was nowhere in sight.

"Wanna talk?" Danica asked.

"There's nothing to say."

"Well, is there something I don't see? I mean, Brad seemed nice enough."

"He is."

Would she ever understand teenagers completely? Danica doubted it.

"So? What's the problem, then? Why not go with them and have some fun? You love the Village."

Michelle shoved her scarf in her pocket and finally lifted her eyes to meet Danica's. "Because, how long would it take before one of the others made fun of me? When they asked if they could come over, and then it'd be all mothballs and Grandma?"

"Hey, Nola is a pretty great grandma, as far as grandmothers go."

Michelle smiled. "Yeah, she is. I don't mean that. But their houses probably smell like cookies in the oven, and their moms are probably all, *Hey, honey, what would you guys like as snacks?*"

"Is that what you think?"

"Even when my mom was home, she wasn't home. She was working, or too tired to move from working too much, or out with some random guy. I have no idea what normal is, but one thing I know is that no one is living like I do." Michelle slumped down on a bench in front of the museum.

"Michelle, these days more than half of marriages end in divorce. Chances are, several of those kids are being raised by one parent, or worse, traipsing from house to house every week, trying to figure out where they belong. This isn't the 1950s. I don't think many moms bake cookies and offer snacks anymore. More likely, moms are working, and when they're home, the kids are on the computer and so are they." She sat down beside Michelle and let out a long breath. "My mom was one of those subservient women. You know, always there, supporting my dad, making cookies, and I have to tell you something that I haven't told anyone else, but I think you need to hear it."

Michelle looked up with interest.

"My father cheated and left her. My own sister can't be happy in a relationship, and we had the perfect mother. She sees my mother as having been weak, staying all those years so her kids would be okay."

"At least she was there."

"Yes, she was there, but there are all sorts of ways to be there and end up hurting your children in the long run."

"Like drinking yourself into oblivion," Michelle said with spite.

"Yes, or like pretending everything is fine when your children know it's not. Or like not working enough to support your kids when the marriage ends." Wow, she hadn't even said those words to Kaylie. What on earth was she doing? Today was not a normal day in any way. "Or having a spouse leave you and your kids end up not trusting anyone—or themselves enough—to have a real, committed relationship." *Belinda. Blake.* "Or worse, sabotaging every chance they have at happiness." *Kaylie. Me? Am I using work as an excuse, even now, while I'm thinking about giving up my license?*

"I guess," Michelle said, but Danica knew she wasn't buying into any of it, even if it was the truth.

"Michelle, you can live your life afraid to move forward, or you can live your life accepting people for who they are and believing in those people, giving second chances with the hopes that the changes they've worked hard to achieve remain. And what they change into might not be your ideal, but it might be close enough that you'll be happy." Danica didn't wait for Michelle's response. "And you don't have to be who others want you to be or who they think you are." *Jesus, am I talking about myself?* "We talked about that, remember? You can be a secure, confident teenager whose mother just happened to fall into the bottle for a bit." *And I can be a therapist who happened to fall for a client.* "And the world will not come to an end. In fact, it just might be better."

213

Danica reached over and pulled on the scarf that was sticking out of Michelle's pocket, then shook it out, and wrapped it around Michelle's neck. She lifted her soft, thick hair, like the woman in the shop had, and she smiled. "There you are again. The happy Michelle."

Michelle grabbed the ends of the scarf. "I do love it." She reached into the neckline of her T-shirt and withdrew the Imperfect necklace. Michelle smiled, rubbing the tin between her fingers and looking into the distance like she was deep in thought.

Danica jumped to her feet, feeling revived. "Where to?"

Michelle reached for the museum door. "Come with me," she said, and Danica followed her into the museum, through the lobby, and toward one of the back rooms.

"Ah, the chaos picture," Danica said, watching Michelle smile at the tangled images.

"Yeah, you know what? I think I figured out why I love it so much." She stepped closer, her neck craning up at the painting. "It reminds me of my life. Remember you asked me that?" She flashed happier eyes at Danica.

Danica nodded.

"Well, I think you were right. All the pieces are there, but they're not in order. That's like my life, isn't it?"

"I suppose you're right." Danica remembered the letter from Nancy. She reached into her purse and pulled it out. "Michelle, please don't be mad, but I went to visit your mom. I wanted to see for myself if she was really making progress before I suggested that you see her."

Michelle's eyes went cold. "And?"

"I think she is. She lives in a nice apartment, and it's filled with your pictures. She's got a job and, well, she asked me to give you this." She held the envelope out toward Michelle.

"What is it?"

"I don't know the specifics." Danica wanted to grant Michelle privacy with regard to the contents of the letter. Whatever her mother had written, she didn't want to dampen or enhance the meaning. That was for Michelle to figure out. "She said she wanted you to have it."

Michelle turned away.

"I'll never push you to see your mom, but I will tell you that everyone makes mistakes, and you two have a whole lot of years ahead of you. I'd just hate to see you throw that away. What she's dealt with is terribly difficult for you, and I don't blame you for not knowing if you can trust anything she says yet."

A couple walked into the room, and Michelle covered her face. The couple wandered back out of the room, and a new trickle of people began to filter in.

"Wanna go?" she asked Michelle.

Michelle shook her head. She took the envelope from Danica and put it in her pocket, then wiped her eyes and forced a smile on her lips. "I don't even know what to think," she said in a hushed voice.

"You don't have to. You're a kid. Just be open to forgiveness if or when you feel it's time." She took Michelle's hand and walked her over to a wooden bench near the corner of the room. They sat side by side. "Michelle, do you remember what it was really like for all those years when your mom was home, or do you think that your memory of her being with random men and drinking was maybe an exaggeration?"

"Here comes Dr. Snow." Michelle smirked.

"I'm sorry. I'm trying to understand something that her counselor told me."

Michelle pursed her lips and looked away.

"Michelle? I won't judge you," Danica assured her.

Michelle crossed her arms. She looked down, around the room, anywhere but at Danica.

"It's okay. We don't have to talk about this." Danica let her off the hook.

They walked around the museum for a few more uncomfortable minutes, and then Michelle asked if she'd take her home. Danica knew she'd caused a setback.

She pulled up in front of Nola's house and apologized to Michelle for prying into her life.

Michelle twisted the ends of her scarf. "I'm not sure how to tell you what I need to say."

Oh God. She doesn't want me to be her Big Sister anymore. Why didn't I see this coming?

"I made most of it up. The stuff I said about my mom not being there, being with random guys and all. I just…"

"Oh, Michelle. I'm so sorry."

"Don't be." Michelle looked up, her voice filled with self-hatred. "I hated her for what she did. I read her diary the night she was drinking, and I know she drank because of my father—who she told me was dead, for God's sake! Dead! She lied to me."

Danica was quick to respond and take control. "She thought it was best, I'm sure."

"Yeah, for her maybe. She wasn't out with random guys. She was never out doing anything other than working, as far as I knew, but then she drank. She drank herself into oblivion that night." Tears spilled from Michelle's eyes. "It was just hard to see—my mother splayed out on her bedroom floor, drunk, totally out of it."

Danica reached for her, and Michelle pushed her away.

"Don't you see? I'm a terrible person. I called her all sorts of names and cursed at her and told her she was worthless as a mother. And the next day, she was gone—in rehab, and I was here with Grandma."

"It was your mother's decision to go into rehab, and I'd imagine, from what I know about your family history, that one night scared her and Nola enough to take it seriously. Alcoholism can be a slippery slope. That's a terrible burden for you to carry, Michelle, but you might have saved her life."

"No, I didn't. I ruined her life. If I hadn't made a big deal of it, she wouldn't have gone into rehab and lost her job; she wouldn't be known as the mom who was an alcoholic. I caused it all. I should have let her have her drunken fit and ignored it, but I couldn't see past my anger because she'd lied to me." Michelle sobbed. "I'm sure you hate me now, and I'll understand if you don't want to hang out with me anymore."

Danica pulled her close this time, not letting Michelle push out of her embrace. "Not see you? You're like family now. You're stuck with me." She hugged her close; then Michelle sank back into the safety of the passenger seat. "I do have one question. Tell me about the first time your mom went to rehab."

"I was little. I don't really remember what happened. I just know I had to stay with Grandma. And I think I used that against her when I found out she'd lied to me about my dad. You should have seen her face when I said she was nothing but a lousy drunk." Michelle's shoulders shook as she sobbed into her hands. "God, I'm so awful."

"No, you were hurt. But why would your mom go into rehab if she didn't have a problem?"

Michelle lifted her pink, puffy face from her hands. "To get away from me."

"Oh, Michelle, you know that's not true."

"I called Grandma, and they argued. I think Grandma made her go, because of what Grandpa was like or something. I don't know."

"What about what the kids at school say about you? Is that true?"

Michelle shrugged.

So, Michelle is transferring her feelings about herself onto everyone else. Great. Danica had to wonder if she was doing the same thing. Did she expect people to judge her for dating Blake, or would they really? Who knew he was her client? Could she be using that as an excuse to distance herself from him? She couldn't explore that now. She had to make sure Michelle was okay.

"What do I do now?" Michelle asked. "I know I shouldn't say it, but I still hate her for lying to me."

"Did you ask her about your father and give her a chance to explain?"

Michelle shook her head. "I read her diary. That was wrong, and I knew it, but I did it anyway. She'll hate *me*."

"I'm not telling you what to do. Only you can make that decision. But sometimes coming clean is the only way to move forward." *Coming clean.* "Holding in feelings can only stagnate you." She reached over and used her index finger to lift Michelle's face so she had to look at her. "What you did was not terrible. Every child reads their parent's diary at some point—when they're living, after they die, out of curiosity. You're not alone in this. Your mom loves you. Let her try to explain; then you can decide whether her reasons are worth hating her forever or not. Maybe they are, maybe not. Who knows?" Danica shrugged.

Michelle nodded, wiped her eyes. "I think you're a really good therapist."

I'm not so sure anymore. "I'm not your therapist," Danica said with a smile.

"Yeah, I know. I'm just sayin'."

Chapter Twenty-Four

Blake spent Sunday at AcroSki, weeding through the mounds of files that Dave had kept track of and trying to figure out what had gone wrong with Danica. He'd thought she would fall into his arms, given the chance. All the signals were there. He'd never felt about any other woman the way he felt about her, and he was sure he read the same message in her eyes. Could he have been that wrong? Had he lost his touch? Damn it. He didn't want to think that way anymore. It wasn't about *his touch*. It was about who he was. She liked him—that was pretty clear—and he liked her. But she wasn't like any other woman. Danica was smart, savvy, and she'd sooner disappear than tie herself up with a guy who played around—a guy like him. *Damn it, Danica!* She'd fucked with his mind and now with his body. Ever since that kiss—that hot, sensual kiss—just thinking about her brought an erection. But he also needed her. Desperately.

When the usual time for his appointment came around, he'd sat and stared at the phone, paralyzed. He fought the urge to call her and apologize. What would he say to her? I'm sorry I made out with you? I overstepped my bounds? I want you? Any way he looked at it, he'd crossed a line, and she was too professional to let that slide. She would never forgive him. First, he elbowed her; then, he kissed her. What the hell was wrong with him? He'd never felt so conflicted about, and drawn to, a woman at the same time. *Shit.* How would he figure out how to handle things with Sally? How could he spend time with Rusty if all he thought about when they were together was that other woman and her son, who had also lost Dave? *Shit.* He should have kept his lips to himself. He really fucked up.

Alyssa peeked into the office. "I'm leaving. Are you okay to close up?"

"Yeah, sure. Thanks for your help," he said.

"Oh, there was some red-haired lady looking for you earlier, but since you said you couldn't be disturbed, I told her that you weren't here."

"Great, thanks." *That's all I would have needed.* Blake realized, as he pondered Red, that more than needing Danica's advice, he missed talking to her. He could have sex with any woman. He wanted more than that with Danica.

"She told me to give you this." She handed him a business card. "It smells like perfume. I think she likes you." She smiled.

Blake took the card and set it on the desk. "Good night, Alyssa," he said.

"See you tomorrow afternoon." Blake was thankful she'd taken on extra hours until he could hire another employee. She closed the door, leaving him alone with his thoughts, a stack of bills, and Red's phone number.

He picked up the card and brought it to his nose, inhaling deeply. He brought his hand to his forehead and closed his eyes. He reached for the phone.

Sally opened the door with a curious look in her eyes. "Blake?"

"Thanks for letting me come over. I really needed to talk to you."

She motioned for him to come in. He followed her to the living room, noting that she didn't look quite as tired as she had the last time they'd spoken. "Can I get you something? You sounded so serious on the phone."

"No, I'm fine." He sat down in an upholstered armchair. He looked toward the stairs. "Is Rusty here?"

Sally shook her head, her ponytail swinging from side to side. "He's out with friends. Listen, if this is about me asking you to spend time with him, I'll understand if you've decided not to."

"That's not it at all. I just...I went to Dave's grave the other day."

Sally cocked her head and drew her nearly transparent eyebrows together.

"I ran into that other woman there. I don't even know her name."

"Trisha," she said, crossing her arms.

You know her name? "Trisha. Okay. I don't know what to say, Sally. I mean, my loyalty is to Dave, but it's also to you and Rusty. I just thought you should know what she told me."

"Blake, listen, you can stop right there."

"But I want you to know. You need to know."

"I already do. She just left a few hours ago. She told me about Chase and about Dave trying to get to know him." Tears filled her eyes. "She said they weren't sleeping together."

"Oh, thank God. That's what she told me, too." Blake felt like his body had been released from invisible shackles. "I was so afraid to tell you."

"She called me and asked if we could talk. I figured it was time to face her, you know? Let her know how I felt about her barging into our lives like she had. But when she came over...She's just this little thing, and she was so scared." She let out a nervous laugh. "I think she was more scared than I was. Anyway, she told me everything, and she said that Dave had been planning to tell me, and I believed her." She let out a relieved sigh. "He did. Actually, he tried once, but I didn't want to hear it. I never let him get far enough to tell me about Chase. I just thought he was spending time with her."

"So, you're okay with it all?" Blake knew then that he would never really understand women.

224

"No. Dave should have told me from the moment he knew, or I should have listened, but I can't change that. The Dave I knew would have done the right thing with regard to the child. I'm glad he did, but I was honest with her. I told her how hurt I was that he'd lied to me and that he'd given her the time that we, as a family, deserved."

Blake ran his hand through his hair as car headlights shone through the front window. Outside, a car skidded to a stop and a car door slammed. "Are you expecting someone?"

She shook her head. "Rusty shouldn't be home for hours yet."

"How'd she take it?"

"She cried. We cried. It's not easy for anyo—"

Rusty came flying through the front door, slamming it behind him. "Mom!" He blew into the living room, red-faced and full of rage. "There you are. And you! Thank God you're fucking here, too."

Blake stood. "Whoa, Rusty." He held his palms up. "Calm down, bud."

"Don't tell me to calm down."

"Rusty Michael, what is wrong with you?" Sally came to her feet, speaking in her sternest, motherly voice. "You don't speak to adults like that."

"No, well, when you hear what I'm about to tell you, you'll be pissed, too. This mother fucker," he said, pointing at Blake, "knew about Dad and that other woman." He turned back toward his mother, nostrils flaring, tears of rage filling his eyes. "That's right. Dad was fucking some other woman, Mom, and that's not all. He has a kid. A fucking kid. Older than me!"

"How did you find out?" Sally's voice trembled.

"My friend Kevin knows a kid who met him."

"Rusty." Blake moved toward him, and Rusty swung at him. Blake grabbed his fist midair. "Whoa! Holy shit, Rusty. Cut it out." He pushed Rusty into a chair, still grasping his fist within his own large hand. "Calm down." He didn't mean to raise his voice, but he couldn't stop himself. He looked at Sally, whose face was streaked with tears; her body trembled as she watched her son fall apart.

"Mom!" Rusty yelled.

Sally came to his side and knelt by the chair. "I know," she said in a soothing voice. "Your father didn't have a mistress, but he did have a child, and the woman you're talking about is the child's mother."

"You knew?" Rusty looked from Blake to Sally and then back again. "What lies did you tell her?" He pushed himself up from the chair, but Blake held him in his seat so he would be forced to listen.

"No. I just found out, and I didn't tell your mother anything. The boy's mother did."

"Jesus fucking Christ, Mom. What the fuck? This is a fucking nightmare." He slumped into the chair, and Blake let go of him, then paced the small room.

Sally shook as she spoke through her tears. "I know, Rusty. I thought he was having an affair, too, but he wasn't. This is a lot to take in."

"A lot to take in? How about this is rewriting fucking history and it sucks!" Rusty yelled.

"Yes, okay, it sucks," she admitted. "But he was your father and he loved you."

"Loved me? The fuck he did. He never spent time with me. He was going to *her* house when I went to practice."

Sally sprang to her feet, her eyes wide with anger. "While you were at practice, Rusty? Really? Do you think I buy that?"

Rusty shot a look at Blake.

"Don't blame him. I knew it when Dad was alive. Your coach called me ages ago. Rusty, your dad let you have your time with your friends—who, I might remind you, you had decided were more important than your family. It was your choice to drop from the team. It was your choice to hang out with your friends and not with us, and I get it, okay? But don't villainize your father any more than he deserves." She wiped her eyes and continued. "Yes, he was spending time at her house with that kid. Yes, he was lying to us about it, but she said that—"

"She said? Why would you believe anything that she had to say?" Rusty demanded.

"Because I love your father, and I'd like to think that I knew what kind of man he was. Because he was getting to know his son and trying to figure out how to tell us about a child who had no choice in the matter about being born. Because if you had been that boy, I'd have hoped for—no, I'd have expected—the same thing of him." Sally sank down into the couch.

Blake was amped up on adrenaline. His eyes darted from mother to son to the front door. He wanted nothing more than to leave them to deal with their issues, but was that appropriate? He wished Danica were there to help him figure it out, but that option was no longer viable. *Danica.* Just the thought of her brought back the taste of their kiss, the feel of her in his arms. If he ever wanted to have a shot with Danica, he had to learn to pull up his big-boy boots and navigate uncomfortable situations. He took a deep breath and forged forward on his own.

"Rusty, I never knew about her or the boy," Blake began.

"Chase," Sally said.

Rusty glared at her.

"He has a name, Rusty, and as hard as it is, he's your half brother. We need to get used to that," Sally said with a pinched look, like the words tasted acidic.

"Like hell," Rusty spat.

"There's plenty of time for you two to deal with all of that," Blake said. "But before I go, Rusty, you need to know that I never knew about any of it. Your dad did nothing but rave about you and your mom. I had no idea that he was spending time with anyone other than the

228

two of you." He started for the door, then turned back, thinking of Danica's wisdom once again. "Listen, this isn't about me. It's about your family, and I get that, but this guy who you want to be angry at, he's not the guy I knew. I don't think I've ever met a guy who believed in family more than Dave." Blake realized that there was no way Dave would have taken his own life. He had even more to live for than Blake had imagined. Blake ran his hand through his hair, distracting himself from the guilt that was gnawing at the muscles in his neck for even considering that Dave could take his own life—and worse, that Dave had been going through so much heartache and turmoil but didn't feel he could confide in Blake. He made eye contact with Sally, once again sure that changing his behavior, becoming a better friend and man, was the most important thing he would ever do. He was beginning to understand how putting others first would change everything for the better. "If you need me, just call."

On the way to his car, Blake knew he had already made a decision about Danica, and there was no way in hell he was going to walk away like a weak boy who had done something wrong. For the first time in his life, he knew he was making the only right choice there was.

Chapter Twenty-Five

It had been weeks since Danica had seen Blake, and as she sat across from Belinda, with her toned-down makeup and less-hookeresque jeans, Danica couldn't help but wonder if Blake had gone back to his player ways.

"Are you listening to anything I'm saying?" Belinda asked.

"Yes, of course. You said you were thinking about taking a writing class." Danica heard the disinterest in her own voice, and it turned her stomach. She needed to pull her shit together. Maybe giving up her career was a good move. Her empathy was failing her, and all she could think about was Blake—not the right thoughts for a therapist to have.

"Yeah," Belinda said in between gum smacks. "I think I have a story to tell. You know, misunderstood woman acts out, then realizes there are other ways to get attention. Who knows. I could be the next E. L. James."

Let's hope not. Danica had picked up James's book at the bookstore, and she'd flinched with embarrassment when a woman at the bookstore saw her reading it. She hoped that if Belinda wanted to be a writer, she wouldn't write something that might be embarrassing for readers to be seen with. *Hell, more power to her if she can write something that sells. Who cares what anyone else thinks.* Danica realized that she'd been thinking that a lot lately. "Maybe so. I think it's a great goal."

"You think I can do it?" Belinda asked.

"I have faith that you can do anything you try to do." After seeing the transitions in Belinda's life, she had even more faith in her.

"Then why are you so glum about it?"

"Am I? I'm sorry. I'm just a little under the weather lately," Danica lied.

"No, you're not. I'd recognize this a mile away. You're bummed over some guy." She laughed. "You went from dressing all professional, to dressing more fun, and now you're back to Little Repressed Annie again." She popped a bubble. "I'm sorry. I probably shouldn't say that."

Caught. "You're...perceptive. But I'm fine, really. And I do think you should write. Writing is very cathartic." *Maybe I should write.*

"Hang in there," Belinda said as she gathered her coat and stood to leave. "In my experience, no guy is worth feeling bad about." She turned and faced Danica with a wide smile across her muted-red lips. "You taught me that." She winked and headed for the door. "See you next week," she called over her shoulder.

The more Danica saw Belinda, the more she liked her, and the more she liked her, the more she saw pieces of her sister in the things she did. It had been weeks since she'd seen Kaylie. She reached for the phone and dialed her number.

"Hello?" Kaylie sounded as if she'd just woken up.

"Hey, you okay?"

"Yeah, just tired."

"Out partying until four in the morning again?" Danica teased.

"No. In fact, I was in bed by ten."

Of course. "Up fooling around till four?"

Kaylie sighed. "What's up, Dan? I've got a gig tonight and need to start getting ready."

She'd almost forgotten that it was Friday. "I miss you. Meet me for lunch tomorrow?"

"Sure, and Camille's wedding is Sunday, so we'll see each other then, too."

The last thing Danica wanted was to go to the wedding and see Blake. She'd kept herself busy enough that she hadn't pined over him since they'd kissed. At least not too much. She had no idea what to expect of her crazy heart when she came face-to-face with him all dolled up in a tuxedo. *Everyone looks handsome in a tuxedo. Crap.* "Yup. Felby's, noon?"

"Great, see you then."

Danica sorted through her files for the coming week, setting a stack to take home and review and another stack to follow up with the clients who were due a phone call. When the phone on her desk rang, she glanced at the clock. It was after five o'clock. Normally, she'd pick up the phone, but she was trying to change that neurotic part of herself, wasn't she? Trying to reclaim some sort of a personal life. She stared at the phone, trying to decide if the pull she felt toward just letting it go to voice mail was another hint that she should think about opening the youth center.

The phone rang on.

The hell with that. Who was she kidding? She had no personal life, and even if she did decide to open the youth center, she still had to be present for her clients until the day she closed her office doors permanently. She reached for the phone. "Hello?"

"Danica?"

Her heart skipped a beat. *Blake.* "Um, yeah. Hi."

"Hi, I'm sorry to bother you. I know you're busy."

Danica listened with her voice caught in her throat.

"I really hate the way things ended, and I'm sorry. Listen, do you think we could meet somewhere and talk?" Before she could answer, he added, "No funny stuff. I promise. I can even come to your office. I just don't feel right about...Well, do you have time?"

Danica quickly scanned her office, searching for an answer that wasn't there. If she met him, she'd be forced to confront her inability to keep work and her own desires separate—even if only this once, with just this one client. It was an admission that she wasn't sure she could face. Facing the truth would definitely mean giving up her career.

"I understand if you don't want to. I mean, it's not like you owe it to me or anything. In fact, I might be asking only so I can clear my own conscience."

What?

"Shit, that didn't come out right. That's not what I meant at all. Look, I can't stop thinking about you. When Monday came around, I sat at my desk and stared into space, wondering what we would have talked about, and I realized that it was *you* I missed talking to, not just the advice you gave me, but *you*."

"Okay." *What are you doing?* She bit her lower lip and turned to look out the window.

"Okay?"

She heard the unexpected enthusiasm in the cadence of his voice. "Sure, we can talk."

"Great, where? When? Want me to come there?"

He sounded like a bumbling boy with a crush, and it made Danica laugh despite her reservations about meeting him. She quickly thought about where they should meet. Someplace public. Someplace where she wouldn't risk letting her emotions take over. Someplace she could test his ability to focus on her instead of the women around her. *This is so wrong. What a bitch to think like that. Shit. What am I doing? Maybe I should forget the whole thing.* "I don't know if this is—"

"Please, don't," he pleaded. "I'm not that guy who walked into your office a few weeks ago. I promise I'm not. Please, just talk to me."

Danica sighed. "Okay." If they met at her office, it would be easier to keep her professional facade.

"Can I take you to dinner?"

Dinner? A date? Am I overthinking? It'd be public. "Um, I'm not sure—"

"Danica, please?"

Danica placed her hand over her racing heart. "Yeah, okay, sure."

"The Embers? Should I pick you up?"

"No, it's okay. I'll meet you there."

"Seven?"

Danica needed some modicum of control. "Eight."

"Okay, then. Eight it is. Thank you, Danica. I'll see you then."

I'm in trouble.

Danica walked the five long blocks to the restaurant, hoping that by the time she arrived, the butterflies in her stomach would get tired of fluttering around. The restaurant came into view, and she stopped to survey her outfit one last time. Beneath her long, quilted coat, she wore a black pencil skirt that ended just above her knees, her favorite Nine West heels—the only ones she didn't mind walking five blocks in—and a white, low-cut blouse. Before she'd left the condo, she'd felt she looked appropriate for an evening business meeting; now, as her heart pounded and her cheeks flushed, she wondered if her skirt was too tight and her blouse too low.

She took a deep breath and hoped the snow that was threatening the night sky would wait until after midnight, as expected. Her hands grew clammy despite the cold air. *It's just dinner with a client. Then why am I worried about my hands suddenly shooting across the table and touching him?* She shoved them in her fur-lined pockets. She concentrated on the sidewalk and approached the entrance to the restaurant.

The Ember's dim lighting sent the butterflies flurrying again. Danica took off her coat, surprised by her trembling hands.

"Party of one?" the hostess asked.

I wish. "No, two. I'm meeting someone here."

The hostess looked at the roster of patrons on the podium before her, then looked up with a smile. "Danica Snow?"

"Yes, that's me." She felt like she was on a blind date. Danica sucked in her stomach and forced a smile.

The hostess turned. "Follow me. Your party is right this way."

She followed the young woman down the restaurant corridor, into the main dining room, and through an archway in the back of the restaurant. Her chest tightened. Every step was like walking in wet concrete.

She clenched her jaw against the urge to flee, and by the time she'd come up with enough excuses to turn and run away—I'm suddenly ill...I left my kettle on—she was standing beside a booth and Blake was coming to his feet, leaning toward her, kissing her cheek.

The hostess put a menu down on Danica's side of the booth. "Enjoy your dinner."

"Thank you," Danica managed. She sat down, trying not to stare hungrily at the opening at the top of Blake's white, button-down dress shirt. He had a ridiculous smile on his lips, and Danica felt a bit like she was on display. She fiddled with her neckline, pulling her blouse across her cleavage, and then watched the shirt slide right back into place, this time knowing the plunging neckline was too revealing. *Great.*

"I'm so glad you agreed to meet me. You look beautiful."

Thank you? Did I say that? Did I think it? Shit.

Blake smiled. "Sorry. I probably shouldn't tell you that." He looked down at the table.

"No, it's okay." *I guess I didn't say it after all.*

He looked back up at her. "I'm sorry. I don't mean for this to be awkward. I wish there was some way we could just pretend that we've just met or something."

Had he read her mind? She was wishing for the same thing. "Maybe that's not a bad idea."

Blake extended his hand across the table. "Hi, I'm Blake Carter. Previous player, ski shop owner, mediocre friend—but I'm working on that."

Danica shook his hand. "Danica Snow, therapist, sister, and, well, I'm probably only a mediocre friend, too." She didn't want to take her hand back. The feel of his soft palm enveloping her slim hand brought a rush of flutters to her stomach. She wondered if the tension behind his eyes was driven by the same heady feeling she was experiencing. Trying to find a balance between desire and appropriateness was not something she was accustomed to. She had never had the problem of business and desire coalescing. But ever since that kiss, Danica had been thinking more and more seriously about letting go of her therapy license altogether and following her dream instead of her parents'.

They both released their grip at the same time. Danica blew out a breath. "Okay, now that the formalities are over..." She heard her therapist voice coming from her lips. Her safe haven. She swallowed that voice and allowed her everyday voice to take over for once. "How have you been?" It took all of her focus not to allow her typical client-therapist follow-up questions to come spewing out of her mouth. "How's Sally?" A safe topic.

Blake flagged over the waitress and ordered a bottle of wine. After the waitress went to retrieve the bottle, he looked a bit more relaxed than he had the moment before. Danica saw the attentiveness in his eyes that she'd noted in the café the first time they'd met—right before he'd looked at the blonde. Now he held her gaze, never wavering toward the attractive waitress or, Danica noted, even turning toward the sounds of three comely women laughing around a small table in the corner of the room. *Chalk one up for Blake.*

Danica listened as he described the scene that unfolded when he'd told Sally about the other woman. "And I guess our town is smaller than I'd ever thought, because Rusty stormed in, armed with information about his father having another son."

The waitress poured them each a glass of wine and took their orders. Danica leaned one elbow on the table, taking in the acceptance in Blake's voice about the revelation that Dave wasn't someone other than what he portrayed. The way he looked at Danica, like she was the only one in the room, pulled her right in.

"Danica, I didn't come to talk about Sally and Rusty."

Danica repositioned herself in her seat. *Me neither.*

"And I didn't ask you to meet me to make you uncomfortable."

Too late. For the first time in her life, she had the urge to kick off her heels under the table and run her toes up the inside of his pant leg. *What on earth is happening to me?* She dug her heels into the carpet beneath her feet.

"I don't know how we went from talking about my life, to," he leaned across the table and spoke softly, "kissing."

Danica was thankful for his apparent respect for their privacy.

"But it did, and I'm not sorry about that. I know I should be, but ever since that day when I whacked your nose, I haven't been able to get you out of my mind."

Danica was usually the direct one. She fiddled with the napkin in her lap, suddenly at a loss for words. She wasn't sorry either, but it *was* wrong. She dropped her eyes, thinking about what she was going to say—what she really felt. Butterflies, wandering toes, and the way she secretly salivated at his touch, took over any restraint she knew she should portray. "I'm not sorry either." She met his eyes and watched them dart from her eyes to her mouth. She lifted her hand and covered her Cindy Crawford mole.

He reached across the table and gently touched her wrist, using pressure so light it was almost nonexistent, to move her hand away from her face. "Don't. You're beautiful. Everything about you is beautiful."

Danica's voice escaped her. *I'm a goner.*

The waitress brought their meals, and they spent the next twenty minutes pushing food around on their plates and making small talk. They finished the bottle of wine and the waitress brought another.

"Oh, no, thank you," Danica said. She was already tipsy, and she didn't want to wake up tomorrow sorry for whatever she might do while under the influence of alcohol. She wasn't Kaylie, after all. Kaylie could pull off the morning-after routine well, but Danica was all flustered words and embarrassment. She lived in the shadow of her profession, worried that someone would find out if she had a sordid one-night stand. She desperately wanted to throw caution to the wind just this once, but her professional persona still held the reins on her mind—even if they were becoming stretched and frayed with each passing second.

"No, I don't suppose we do," Blake agreed. He set his napkin on the table and leaned back. "Are you up for a walk?"

A kiss or a walk? Jesus, Danica.

They walked toward town as snow began to fall. At first it was just a few light flakes, but within ten minutes they were walking amid a thick winter storm, which was not unusual for Colorado. Danica and Blake walked side by side, hands shoved deep in their pockets. They neared the center of town, where a brick, circular patio hosted ornate, iron benches.

Blake stopped beneath one of the old-fashioned streetlights. "Wanna head back to my car?" Blake asked.

That was the last thing Danica wanted to do. Walking beside Blake helped to settle her fluttering stomach. The crisp air revitalized her, freezing her worry about what she might do and replacing it with a modicum of ease. Outside, she was free and there was room to breathe. In a car, she'd be trapped. She stole a glance at his profile. With his angular nose and snow-spotted hair, he could be a model, shot in a commercial for some manly cologne. God, he was gorgeous. He caught her looking, and this time she didn't look away.

Her heart thundered in her chest. Her nerves tingled with desire, and it was as if she had no control over her muscles. She was powerless to turn away.

He stepped toward her, his breath visibly meeting the air between them. Their breath comingled into little puffs of white that evaporated into the night. "State of Grace" by Taylor Swift played loudly from a passing car.

That's it. You *are my Achilles' heel, Blake Carter. Goodbye, career.* Danica stepped toward him, snow falling across her nose. Taylor Swift faded into the distance. *I never saw you coming. And I'll definitely never be the same.* Their lips met in a long, delicious kiss. Her arms circled his neck. He put his hands on her lower back, sending a tantalizing rush through her body. Never before this had she felt she was in the exact right moment at the exact right time. His tongue moved slowly inside her mouth, the sweet taste of wine alighting her senses. She pressed her body against him, feeling his need in his touch. His fingertips traveled up her back, beneath her hair, to the sensuous spot behind her ear. He kissed her until her body was filled with warmth instead of her head filled with thoughts. His lips found her chin, then her neck. *Bliss.* The world fell away. The street noises grew silent, save for the sound of her own sweet breath as he drank her in. She reached down and brought his lips back to hers, running her tongue along them, tasting the sweet wine and the salty desire that lay beneath.

"Danica," he whispered.

"I know," she said between kisses. Danica's heart pounded against her ribs, as if it might explode. In that split second, she made a decision that she knew there was no turning back from. "My place." She took his hand, and they hurried through the falling snow like teenagers, laughing and kissing every few steps. When they reached her condo, Danica fumbled in her purse for the keys as Blake kissed the back of her neck. He spun her around and kissed her, pressing his hips against hers and her back against the door. Heat electrified her body. She pushed him away and fumbled for her keys, unlocking the door as quickly as she could. She yanked him inside by the collar, then shut the door, thrusting him against it with a passionate kiss. Danica felt as though she were falling into quicksand—and loved every blessed second of it.

She fumbled with the buttons on his shirt, her lips trailing down his magnificent, muscular chest. She could barely catch her breath. She licked the soft skin just above his belt and worked it free, unzipping his pants as a moan escaped his lips.

He slid his hand under her chin and lifted her face to look up at him. He shook his head. "Not like this," he whispered.

Danica felt as if she'd been punched in the gut, her heart shattering into a million little pieces. She'd given herself to him and he was pushing her away?

He took her hand in his, kissing the tips of each of her fingers, and lifted his eyes to the stairs.

Oh, thank God. A smile replaced her fears. She kissed him again, then led him upstairs to her dark bedroom. Once she let him in, there was no going back. Danica stood by the bed, battling her conflicting emotions for only a second before accepting that she could not turn him away. Her body begged for him; her heart had already let him in. She would not turn him away. He unbuttoned her shirt slowly, stopping between each button and touching her skin lightly with his fingertips. When he reached her navel, he lowered his lips and licked tiny circles along her skin, sending heat between her legs. She took a step toward the bed, and he held on tight to her hips, not letting her lower herself down. His tongue trailed up her center to the clasp in her bra. He used his fingers and unclasped it. Danica shivered as her breasts broke free.

"I don't want to rush this," he whispered, dropping her blouse from her shoulders.

Danica's chest heaved up and down with each breath. She couldn't think past her desire to touch him, but her hands were trapped against her sides by her blouse. She stood, half naked, trembling beneath his touch and growing hotter by the second.

He moved his tongue to her nipples, gently licking around them until she thought she might scream. He took her breast into his mouth and rolled his tongue lightly across her nipple; then he drew away and pulled her blouse from her arms, dropping it to the ground beside them. The shock of cold air intensified her desire.

Habit took over, and she moved to cover her stomach.

"Uh-uh," he said, and kissed her sides, sending a tickle right through her.

He came to his full height and slipped out of his shirt. She touched his chest, running her fingers along the ridges of his pectoral muscles, shivering inside at the sensuality of him. Blake ran his hands under her thick hair and palmed her skull, tilting her head back. He kissed her neck until her legs felt like rubber and her thoughts ran together. Then he lifted her within his arms and laid her gently on the bed, where he kissed his way down her neck, to her breasts, her sternum, and her belly button, where his tongue lingered. She slithered out of her skirt, and he from his slacks. She lay beneath him, wanting him inside her, wanting to feel his bare chest against hers, her heart beating in time to his.

He lowered his lips to hers. "Danica," he whispered. "You are so beautiful." He repositioned himself so he was lying next to her, his arm over her chest, his erection against her thigh. He breathed hard and fast, leaning on one arm, looking down at her. "I just don't want this to be something it's not."

Her heart shattered again. She sucked in a gasp of air.

"You're not a one-night stand. This is real. Do you feel that way, too? Before we go any further, I have to know."

She pulled him on top of her and guided him between her legs. "You are anything but a one-night stand."

He rested his forehead on hers.

"I don't even know how to have a one-night stand," she admitted.

"And I never will again." He kissed her hard as he slid inside of her.

Chapter Twenty-Six

Waiting for Kaylie was like waiting for it to snow in Florida, and Danica had been waiting for her for twenty-seven years. She checked her watch again. Kaylie was fifteen minutes late. What else was new? She flagged down the waitress and ordered iced teas for them both—and not the benign kind. Today she needed alcohol. It wasn't every day she confessed her deepest sins to her little sister.

The middle-aged couple at the next booth held hands across the table. Danica noticed their wedding bands and wanted that safety, that comfort. Finally, after years of being the proper one and not letting herself do anything that might not be seen as becoming of a therapist, she'd let herself relax into the most sinfully delicious night of passionate sex she'd ever experienced. Beneath Blake's touch, she became a different person. She allowed herself to try things she'd heard Belinda and

Kaylie talk about, using her body in ways that she'd imagined only sleazy people might. But there was nothing sleazy about what she and Blake had—she knew that with every fiber of her being. She couldn't understand the hows and whys of them ending up together, or the night they had shared, but as she thought about his touch, the feel of his tongue lingering on her skin, the taste of him in her mouth, her legs tingled and her body shuddered with aftershocks that were almost as thrilling as the original orgasms.

Kaylie flounced through the door in her crushed-cotton skirt and T-shirt, carrying an armful of colorful shopping bags. Every eye in the café was drawn to her, like metal to magnet, male and female alike. She dropped the shopping bags next to the booth and sat down, oblivious to the attention.

For once, Danica didn't pull her sweater around her middle, feeling second fiddle. She didn't try to fix her hair or cast her eyes down to the table. *One night really can change everything.*

"Hey, sis." Kaylie wiggled into the seat across from her, shaking her perfect, little C cups and surveying the people in the next booth. She smiled when the man looked over. Danica wondered if Kaylie noticed—or cared about—his wife's sneer. "Sorry I'm late."

Right. Danica wanted to be mad at her for being late, but ever since her evening with Blake, and the good morning kiss he'd planted on her lips, she'd been unable to harbor anything but joy. "No worries. I knew you might be, so I ordered us drinks. Iced teas."

Kaylie's eyes lit up; then she peeked into the bright pink Victoria's Secret bag. "So, what's the dealio?"

Danica's usual annoyance at how cute Kaylie sounded when she used slang was gone. Her entire outlook had changed overnight. She was happy for Kaylie's silly, little mannerisms. Maybe she'd been too judgmental of her sister all along. Maybe her criticisms were there because she, herself, wasn't happy. Danica mulled over the truth of her thoughts. She had to tell Kaylie about Blake. No, she wanted to tell her. She deserved to know. *Ease into it.* Danica wasn't sure if Kaylie would hate her or cheer her on.

"I just thought we could catch up. I guess I just miss seeing you." *Are those bags under her eyes?* Kaylie was acting like her peppy self, but her eyes were anything but peppy. Danica wondered what was up.

Kaylie whipped a pink thong from her bag. "Look what I got. Isn't it cute?" She held it up between her index fingers and thumb, her pinky stuck up like Vanna White presenting a prize.

Kaylie pushed her hair behind her ear. A wayward curl sprang free. Although Kaylie was acting like her effervescent self, Danica saw fatigue in the lines around her eyes.

"Are you all right, Kay? What's been going on the last few days? You look tired."

"I've been tired." She shrugged.

Not a surprise with your sex life. The waitress brought their drinks, and Danica tried to figure out how she would tell Kaylie that she'd slept with Blake. Kaylie had called dibs on him, but that thought had been nowhere near her mind last night. She checked the time again. She had two hours before meeting Blake, and she promised herself she'd tell Kaylie. Danica had no desire to sneak around or pretend she wasn't with him at the wedding, but she didn't relish telling Kaylie that she'd ignored her dibs for the first time in her life.

"Kay, who are you chasing now? What happened to that other guy?" *God, what is his name?* "Chaz?" It seems like yesterday when they'd been behind the closed door of their childhood bedroom, lying on the floor, head-to-head, Kaylie talking about which base she let her latest boyfriend get to and Danica trying to convince her that she shouldn't be letting boys touch her. My, how the tables had turned. Danica was the one ready to kiss and tell.

"Chaz?" Kaylie swatted the air and feigned a laugh. She looked away and swallowed hard.

Shit. Something's off.

"He was fun, but..." Kaylie took a big gulp of her drink; then her eyes grew wide. "Oh! Iced tea! I thought you meant the nonalcoholic iced tea." She pushed it away.

"Not drinking?"

Kaylie shrugged. "Tired. Chaz wanted to get serious, and, well—" She shrugged, scrunching her face in that adorable way she had that made guys swoon and girls cringe.

"What's wrong with that? Don't you want a steady boyfriend instead of running around all the time?"

"Yes. No. I'm not sure," she said. Kaylie pulled her foot up and put it underneath her other leg, laying her hand across her stomach.

"I don't get it. I mean, Chaz is drop-dead gorgeous and he treats you well. Isn't that what you said?" Kaylie went through men like puppies went through shoes— fast and furious—then tossed them away, damaged and heartbroken.

She twisted a curl around her finger. "Maybe I want someone else." She wrinkled her nose. "Blake, maybe." When she said it, it came out like a dream, silky and untouchable. "I think he's different. I think there's more to him than just the hunky man I want to pounce on."

Danica's stomach lurched. *Down girl. Put your claws away.* "Wha—what makes you think that?"

"Well, for one thing, he didn't go home with me that night."

Thank God for little favors.

"Hard to get. I like that," she said.

"What about asking if you could take a date to the wedding? What was that all about?" *Careful. Don't hurt her.* "Kaylie, why do you always sabotage the good relationships in your life?"

"Don't get all therapisty with me, Danica." The spark in Kaylie's eyes faded. "I was gonna take Chaz, but I don't know. I think I need some space. I'm not the commitment type."

"Only because you decided that you aren't. You're beautiful, smart, and lovable. Why Blake? He's not your type." *Anymore.*

"Maybe not, but at least I won't end up like Mom."

"Kaylie, stop it. You aren't Mom. Chaz isn't Dad." *Blake is mine!* "Talk to me, Kaylie. What's really going on?"

With that, tears sprang from Kaylie's eyes. "Can we talk about something else, please?" Kaylie called over the waitress and asked for ice water. She wiped the tears from her eyes and changed the subject. "The wedding is tomorrow. You're ready?"

"Of course I'm ready. Aren't you?" *What the hell is going on?* Kaylie had been ready weeks ago.

Kaylie fiddled with her napkin. "My dress is being let out. I have no idea why, but it's a little tight." She looked at Danica with a feigned smile across her lips and her hand across her stomach. "Gotta watch that or no one will want me."

"You're more than your looks, Kaylie. You have a line of suitors that would wrap around this building twice. What on earth is really going on with you?"

Kaylie didn't answer.

Danica's phone buzzed with a text. She read the message from Blake: *Miss you. Can't wait to kiss you.* She turned off the phone and tucked it into her purse, her heart thundering in anticipation.

"I don't know. I've just been so emotional lately. Hormones or some shit, I guess."

Danica took a gulp of her iced tea. She had to tell her. She couldn't let the charade go on much longer.

"After the wedding, you know how Camille said we could change into something more comfortable than those awful bridesmaid gowns?" Kaylie pushed her hair behind her ear.

"Yeah."

"I'm wearing that little black number I bought the other week, the thong," she lifted her eyebrows, "and...I wanted to borrow those slinky, black, stiletto boots you have."

My fuck-me heels? She'd been wearing them the night she ran into Blake at the bar. The night that Kaylie and Danica had first been introduced to him. The night Kaylie had turned to Danica and said, "Dibs." Guilt thickened around Danica's chest. *No,* Danica though. *I'm not going to feel guilty about being happy.*

Kaylie grabbed Danica's hand across the table. "Pretty please? I'll be really careful with them."

Danica couldn't deny her. Kaylie was still her younger sister, and she knew Blake would never betray her, so why not? Her lips lifted into a smile as she soaked in that thought: Blake would never betray her. "Okay, but be careful. If one little—"

Kaylie half stood and pulled Danica across the table into a tight hug. "Oh, thank you! Thank you! I'm sure to get noticed now! I'll come by around six thirty."

Shit.

Chapter Twenty-Seven

"Why don't we tell her together?" Blake lay on Danica's bed, leaning against the pillow, the lower half of his body still wrapped in her comforter.

Danica sat on the edge of the bed, pulling on her jeans. "You can't be here when she gets here. That would be too awkward, and there's no way I'd ever make a scene at the wedding." She slipped her T-shirt over her head and turned to face him, desperately wanting to melt right back into his arms. "Besides, she's my sister. I have to tell her in the right way."

"I'll do it," he said in a cocky voice. "How hard can it be?"

"She bought a pink thong for you." Danica smirked.

"Really? And why do I want to turn her away again?"

She threw a pillow at him and he caught it midair, then sprang up and tackled her on the bed, kissing her

257

neck and pawing at her breasts. She playfully pounded on his back.

"You're such an ass," Danica kidded. In the past, she never would have gone anywhere near a man that Kaylie had called dibs on. Her insecurities would have run wild: *Is she prettier than me? Would you ever leave me for her? Are you trying to get to her through me? I'm not as fun as she is.* With Blake, those questions came nowhere near her lips.

He laid the full weight of his chest on Danica, looking seriously, sensuously, into her eyes. If Danica were a hopeless romantic, she might liken the way he stared right into her soul to love, but she knew better. Great sex and an insatiable desire to be together for twenty-four hours did not equate to love. *Did it?*

He kissed her head and whispered, "I started writing that list you asked me to."

"Really?"

"Yeah. So far, what I like about myself is you." He kissed her cheek. "You'll tire of this, you know," he said.

"Never."

"Sneaking around. Hidden texts. That's not who you are, and honestly, that's not who I am anymore, either." He sat up. "Just tell her."

Danica turned away so he wouldn't see her blush. She'd never been the one sneaking around before, and she had to admit that it did heighten the intrigue. The clock read 6:15. "Shit. You gotta go." She pushed him off of the bed and jumped to her feet. Danica grabbed his jeans from the floor and tossed them to him. "Here. Put these on. She'll be here in fifteen minutes, and you can't be here."

"Okay, okay. Sheesh. Use me and toss me away." He stuck out his lower lip in a supreme pout.

"Shut up," she said with a grin. "Just hurry up. The last thing we need is to have a big blowup tonight." *Or end up back in bed before she gets here.* "I'll tell her when you're not here."

He cocked his head and furrowed his dark eyebrows.

"I promise, okay?"

Blake wrapped her in his arms and kissed her hungrily. Danica's mind headed for the clouds. She no longer felt like Danica, Proper Therapist, but rather like a happier version of herself. Danica, Lovesick Woman *and* Therapist. She *would* tell Kaylie. There was no way she would mess up their relationship, or whatever it was.

When he finally released her, she was breathless and full of desire.

"Can I come back after she leaves, or do you have a hot date?" he asked.

A knock at the front door pulled Danica from her musing over the possibilities of what later might hold.

"Shit. She's early." She frantically gathered his shoes and socks and shoved them in his hands. "Take these. Go out the back. Please."

Blake sat on the bed, calm as a lily soaking up sun, a wide grin spread across his stubble-ridden cheeks. "This could be interesting."

"You wish." She grabbed his arm and yanked him to his feet. He came up slowly to his full height, his chest a millimeter from her face. He placed his hands on either side of her face and kissed her again—hard. Then, he planted gentle kisses on her cheeks, forehead, and neck. Danica closed her eyes, taking in the scent of him and the feel of his palms on her face, and relishing in the warmth that spread through her body.

"I'll be back," he whispered.

She snagged a piece of licorice from the bedside table and gnawed on it while watching him walk out onto the balcony. He blew her a kiss and then disappeared down the back steps. *Living in a town house has its advantages.*

"Danica!" Kaylie pounded on the front door.

Having a sister has its disadvantages.

Danica pulled the door open, and Kaylie breezed by in a skintight, black dress that hugged her curves from the spaghetti straps on her narrow shoulders to the lacy hem that landed mid-thigh.

"What the hell, Dan? I was freezing out there." She crossed her arms, fuming at Danica. Her mask of anger fell away and her eyes grew big.

Danica felt her chest and neck flush with heat.

"Oh. My. God," she said, her arms falling to her sides. "Licorice?" She headed for the stairs.

"Wait, Kaylie!" Danica took the stairs two at a time behind her as Kaylie sprinted toward her bedroom.

Sisters in Love

"Hello?" Kaylie called out in a singsong voice.

Danica caught up to her at her bedroom door, which she had thankfully closed.

Kaylie mouthed, "Who's in there?" and pointed to the door.

"No one." Danica pushed the last bit of licorice into her mouth, chewing too fast to savor the cherry flavor.

"Uh-huh. You only eat licorice after sex. What did you used to call it? The perfect little after-party for your mouth?"

They both laughed. Danica hadn't called it that since she was in college, though she still believed it to be true. Kaylie pushed open the door and they both stood there, waiting for someone to appear. Kaylie stared with wonder as the door moved in slow motion to expose an unmade bed and Danica's bra on the floor. Danica closed her eyes and held her breath.

Kaylie walked into the bedroom. "Well, well, well, which of the three bears was in here?" She spun around to face Danica with a snicker on her lips.

"No one. It's the middle of the afternoon." Danica pulled at her sheets, nervously making the bed. "I just didn't have time to clean up before you came over."

"You can't fool me, sis. I see it in that hazy look in your eyes. Shit, I can smell sex in this room. Open a window, for God's sake."

Danica's jaw dropped open.

Kaylie's finger wagged in her face. "Aha! Got ya!" Kaylie roared with laughter. "Who was it? Jonathan? Or, that really hot bartender? Or..."

Danica bit her lower lip and counted to three, mustering the courage to face her sister—and her confession. She gently touched Kaylie's forearm. "Kaylie," she said.

Kaylie silenced and stared at her expectantly.

Silent seconds stretched between them. Danica was about to break her sister's heart and maybe her trust. Damn, was she? What right did Kaylie have to place dibs on a man, anyway? She could have any guy she wanted. She'd be over Blake in a heartbeat.

"What?" Kaylie looked at the clock and headed for Danica's closet. "Oh shit, forget it. I gotta get ready for my gig tonight. Where are those boots?" She crossed the bedroom, passing the armchair with the olive-green throw tossed over the back, passing the stack of books on the floor, and their grandmother's wooden wall mirror.

Danica gathered courage with every step her sister took. She watched Kaylie bend down to pick up the boots from the closet floor, her thong outlined by the slinky dress. She had to tell her. She couldn't take another minute of knowing her sister wanted her man, and more importantly, she couldn't watch Kaylie throw away someone who loved her for someone she'd never have.

"I'm sleeping with Blake." The words spilled from Danica's mouth.

Kaylie remained in that bent-over position as if she hadn't heard her. Her fingers hovered over the heels she'd been searching for.

"Kay?" Danica waited for her to throw herself at her, yell at her about how she had *dibs* or some other utterly ridiculous claim she assumed was viable. Kaylie didn't move. "Kaylie, I'm sorry. I didn't plan it. In fact, I tried not to let it happen." *Okay, maybe that wasn't exactly true, but I thought about not letting it happen.*

She watched Kaylie's shoulders sag. Danica imagined her closing her eyes, willing away the tears, and it broke her heart. Why did her happiness have to be with someone Kaylie had set her sights on?

Kaylie turned around slowly, leaving the heels on the closet floor. "You slept with Blake?" There was no hurt in her eyes, no cold, hard stare, only the question that came softly from her lips.

"Mm-hmm." *Shit.*

"You and Blake?" She walked toward Danica. "Sexy, dark-haired, muscular, turned-me-down Blake?" She raised her eyebrows, planting herself inches from Danica.

Danica took a step backward. Kaylie was typically upbeat or angry—but never dead calm. Dead calm rattled Danica's nerves. She grasped at finding the right words. "He...we...it just happ—"

"Just happened. I get it." Kaylie walked around Danica and sat on the edge of the bed. "Well, things happen."

Who are you? "Kaylie? Aren't you mad at me?"

Kaylie shook her head.

"Thank God." She sat next to her sister. "Because I think I'm really falling for him."

Kaylie turned a thin smile toward her sister. "I'm happy for you."

"Then why are you acting like you're catatonic?"

Tears slipped down Kaylie's cheeks. "Because I'm pregnant."

Danica's jaw dropped. "Pregnant?"

Kaylie nodded.

"But how? Who? Yesterday you were saying that you wanted to hook up with Blake." *What the hell?*

"It's Chaz's." Kaylie stood and paced. "I'm scared, Danica. I don't know what to do. I have been trying to ignore it—hoping it would go away."

"Oh, Kay." Danica went to her and hugged her close. Feeling her sister's sobs against her shoulder brought tears to her eyes. "What are you gonna do?"

Kaylie pushed away and shook her head. "I keep telling myself I need to abort the baby. I can't be a mom. I can't *be* Mom."

Danica's therapist senses went into overdrive. As she felt that familiar rush of adrenaline, she realized that very soon she'd no longer be playing the role of therapist, and that thought comforted her. "Can't be a mother, or can't be *our* mother?"

Kaylie sat back down on the bed, covering her face with her hands. "I don't know. I'm scared to death. What if Chaz leaves me like Dad left Mom?"

Damn it, Dad! "Okay, let's take this apart and figure it out. Do you love him?"

"I do. I really do. I'm just scared to death."

"Okay, that's good." She patted Kaylie's leg. "Wait. Does he know?"

Kaylie nodded. "He asked me to marry him."

"Kaylie, I want you to really think about this, because this is not some game. This is not a decision to take lightly. Whatever you do will impact far too many people to make the wrong choice." Danica breathed in deeply and let it out fast. "Do you love him enough to be with only him...forever?"

"I didn't think I could. That's why I was thinking about seducing Blake. If I'm gonna blow it, might as well blow it with the hottest guy around."

Danica cringed.

"But I realized, as I was getting dressed today and thinking about singing tonight, that—oh yeah, did I tell you Chaz and I are fighting? He won't be at my gig tonight. He wants to get married, but I told him I had to think about it. Anyway, I realized that I don't want to do the gig if he's not there. I don't want to go to bars and pick up guys, but I'm not sure I can be loyal. What if I'm like Dad? What if that's why I've been...like I've been for so long?"

Danica had to be careful. She knew Kaylie was vulnerable enough to follow any direction that Danica pointed her in. Instead, she'd give her the facts and let her sister make the most important, and probably the most painful, decision of her life.

"Kaylie, you're like you are *because* of Dad, not because you're like Dad."

"Yeah?"

"Yeah. You're afraid of commitment, but not incapable of commitment. You're afraid of being blindsided, like Mom was. That's why you try to do it first."

"Oh God, really? I do that? That's awful."

"No, it's not. It's called self-preservation." She knelt in front of Kaylie, placed her hands on her knees, and looked into her confused and sad eyes. "What does your heart tell you to do? And, Kaylie, you don't have to make a decision today."

"I'm eight weeks pregnant. I have to make a decision soon." She burst into tears and fell sideways on the bed, burying her face in the pillow.

"You have weeks to decide, not seconds. Remember when you were little and you couldn't decide between chocolate and vanilla?" She lay down next to Kaylie, her hand on her back. "Dad told you that you had to choose, and you said—"

"That my heart would choose, but my brain didn't have to," Kaylie said into the pillow. "Follow my heart?"

"Right. What does your heart say?"

"Every time I think about *not* having this baby, I fall apart. But I'm afraid to love Chaz. I don't think I can stand being hurt like Mom was."

"But do you think you love him?"

Kaylie turned her red-rimmed eyes toward Danica. "I know I love him."

"Yeah?"

Kaylie nodded, swiping at the tears that stained Danica's pillow. "You really don't think I'm like Dad? You don't think I'll wake up one day and not want my family anymore, or find some other guy too attractive to turn down?"

Danica lay on her back and stared up at the ceiling, taking Kaylie's hand in her own. "Have you ever met a man and thought that you couldn't live without bedding him? Or do you bed them because they're there and you're bored, or because you want to bed them before some other girl in the bar does?"

"You sound like a therapist again."

"I know," Danica said quietly. "This time I have to. I want you to think about your answers, and you don't have to tell me. You only have to be honest with yourself." Warmth spread through Danica. She'd watched Kaylie standing at the edge of a precipice for so many years, and now she was finally able to help—if only a little. Now it was all up to Kaylie. She could have her happily ever after if she so desired, and if not, Danica would be there to help her pick up the pieces—like always.

Kaylie put her head on Danica's shoulder.

"No matter what you decide, I'll support your decision."

Chapter Twenty-Eight

Danica leaned over the kitchen counter, watching Blake eat breakfast. She couldn't believe how much her life had changed and how freeing it was to allow herself to live outside the shadow of her profession. So what if people talked? Who would know he was her client, anyway? As she mulled it over, she realized that she'd already made her decision. What she felt was love—thick, unavoidable, spectacular love. She was going to relinquish her therapy license and find a way to open the youth center she'd always dreamed of. It was time to stop living how other people wanted her to, and, instead, live the life that would make her the happiest. Looking at Blake, she knew she'd made the right decision.

"Aren't you gonna eat anything?" Blake stood and went to her. He wrapped his arms around her and whispered in Danica's ear. "Dr. Snow, I think I might need a private session."

She placed her hand on his unshaven cheek. "I'm not going to be Dr. Snow for much longer. I've decided to open the youth center I've always dreamed of."

"And leave the safety net you've spent so many years constructing?" Blake asked.

"Look at you, all attune to someone else's issues. You must have had a very good therapist." Danica pressed her hips in to his. "It's not just the right thing to do. It's what I want to do. I've just never had the courage to let myself move in that direction before." She kissed his cheek. "See, you've helped me grow as much as I've helped you. Oh gosh. I have to go meet Michelle."

He kissed her softly, pressing his hips in to hers. "I would never interfere with your plans. Michelle is lucky to have you in her life, and the youths of Allure will be equally as lucky."

Blake and Danica had stayed up half of the night talking about Kaylie and what it had been like for Danica, living in her shadow. While she reminisced, she realized that she hadn't been living in Kaylie's shadow at all. She was living right beside her, but always with a watchful eye and a modicum of jealousy wrapped in worry. She told Blake about Michelle's mother and how hurt Michelle was over the lies about the father she never knew. Blake had turned to her with an earnest look in his eyes and said, "I will never lie to you. I've seen the wake of hurt Dave left behind, and I'd rather face an argument than ever have you feel like you weren't the most important thing in my life."

I love you crossed her mind, but not her lips. *Baby steps.*

"So, what should I do when I need advice? Make an appointment? Leave you a note? Call you *Doc*?" He laughed.

"Hmm. I'll have to see if I can fit you in around the kids' schedules, I suppose." She laughed. "How about just saying, 'I need a little advice'?"

"Sounds good to me. Did I tell you that Sally called me? She said that Rusty agreed to talk to someone with her, a counselor."

"That's great news. Maybe he can even spend time at the new youth center when it's open." Danica knew the road ahead for Dave's family—families—would be a long one.

"Yeah. It's a start, anyway. Oh, and I'm taking Rusty next weekend. Maybe we can bring Michelle and all go to a movie." He lifted his eyebrows.

"Listen to you. A matchmaker."

"No. I was selfishly thinking of necking in the back of the theater." He laughed, then looked at the clock and gulped down his last sip of coffee. "I have to get to AcroSki. I'm interviewing a part-timer today to take over a few of the administrative things Dave had been in charge of. Are we driving to the wedding together?"

They'd become so close over the last forty-eight hours that it felt to Danica as if they'd been a couple for years. She'd already assumed they would go to the wedding together. It was a little surprising to realize that

271

there was a whole world of people who didn't know they'd found each other. "I wouldn't want it any other way."

Danica drove into the Village with Michelle, humming along to a Top 40s radio station. Michelle wanted to go to a particular used bookstore to look at inexpensive art books, which Danica took as a good sign. Michelle was showing interest in something other than hiding behind her imaginary wall.

"You're wearing that blue scarf again," Michelle noticed.

Danica touched the scarf. "Yeah."

"You look really nice. Happy," Michelle said.

"Yeah? Thank you. I am." Danica shivered, thinking of being wrapped in Blake's arms.

Danica pulled into a parking spot and they headed for the bookstore. "You like being here, don't you?"

"In the Village? Yeah, a lot. It's so different from being in town." Michelle reached into the neckline of her shirt and withdrew her Imperfect necklace, patting it against her chest. "I've been thinking about what you said about my mom."

They walked up the steps to the bookstore and stood on the brick stoop. Michelle brushed her hair from her eyes and looked thoughtfully at Danica. The difficulties in her life showed in the shadows within her eyes.

"Maybe if I talked to her it would, I don't know, help."

Danica wanted to jump up and down and clap her hands. Instead she spoke calmly. "I think it will. You know I'd be happy to come with you if you want me to."

Michelle nodded and pulled open the door.

Before following her inside, Danica looked up at the sky and breathed in the cool air. Everything in her life was finally coming together. If she had her therapist hat on, she might become cynical and tell herself to be prepared for the next shoe to drop. She smiled to herself, knowing that soon the therapist side of her mind wouldn't always have to be on high alert. She refused to let her practical side overtake her happiness. She knew the risks; Blake could go back to his player ways at any moment. He might become bored. He might resent her for trying to change him—no, that last one wasn't true. Blake had come to her wanting to change. She replaced her therapist's eye view with that of her normal, womanly self, tucked the thought into her heart, and walked into the bookstore.

An hour later, they left, Michelle armed with various art books and Danica armed with two books about pregnancy—just in case Kaylie decided to move in that direction.

She dropped Michelle off at Nola's house. After Michelle went inside, Danica felt a familiar constriction in her chest. Disappointment. Michelle hadn't brought up talking to her mother again, as Danica had hoped she would. She checked her watch. She had two hours before she had to be at the church for the pre-wedding pictures.

Correction: She and Blake needed to be there in two hours. Her pulse quickened as she headed home.

Chapter Twenty-Nine

The chilly evening air blew through Blake's hair as he stood on Danica's front stoop and watched the sun disappear behind the mountain. His palms sweated, despite the thirty-degree temperature. His stomach swam in circles for the first time in years. Blake turned as Danica met him on the porch, locking the door behind her. Shades of mauve swayed in the breeze beneath the hem of her coat. Blake gasped a breath at the sight of her. How could one woman look more beautiful every time he saw her? Her natural curls blew across her face, and she laughed as she tried unsuccessfully to tame them with her hand.

"They have a mind of their own," Danica joked.

"They're gorgeous. You are gorgeous." He kissed her on the lips, once, twice. Then he couldn't help it; he pulled her to him and let his passion lead him into another insatiable kiss.

She came away with her cheeks flushed.

"I'm sorry, but..." He shrugged, hoping he could control the heat that found its way to his groin.

Hand in hand, they walked to the car, where Blake opened the door for Danica, feeling like an overeager teenager taking the hottest girl to prom. After closing her door, he stood in the cold watching her smooth her dress. He felt his heart swell in a way he had never before experienced, and thought of Dave and Sally. Their relationship might have been going through a hurricane, but somehow Blake thought that had the accident never occurred, they would have weathered the storm. Even though he and Danica were only in the early stages of their relationship, she already owned a piece of Blake's heart, and he couldn't imagine losing her.

Danica turned to pull her seat belt across her chest and caught him staring. She wrinkled her forehead in question. He hurried into the driver's seat as Danica read a text on her cell phone.

"They didn't call off the wedding, did they?"

Danica read the text from Michelle. *Will you come with me to talk to my mom tomorrow?* She typed *yes* into the phone. "No," she answered Blake. "Everything is just perfect."

They stood across from each other during the wedding ceremony. Blake with the groomsmen, beaming in their tuxedos, and Danica alongside the bridesmaids, lined up like brightly colored flowers, beautiful and enticing.

Camille looked lovely in her satin gown, but what struck Danica was the look in her eyes. She and Jeffrey had been dating for three years, and there was no way to describe how she looked at him other than *dreamy*. Her cheeks were soft, her eyes attentive, and her body language emitted simple and pure love. Her shoulders faced Jeffrey's, her posture straight, yet slightly leaning toward her future husband, and her lips were slightly parted, turned up at the edges in a wanting, comfortable smile. She and Jeffrey had written their own vows, and Danica listened intently to Camille's promise: *...to always consider your feelings, to give you time to nurture your friendships, and to try not to jump to unfair conclusions.* She'd never heard such thoughtful vows. What would she hope for from a spouse? Danica had never given marriage much thought. She hadn't had time, and love had left almost everyone she knew in some state of mental chaos. Fate had never existed in her world—until now. Now she felt the delicate fingers of love lacing themselves around her heart, and she was helpless to ignore them. She wondered if Blake felt the same, and glanced up at him. He was looking directly at her, with that same look in his eyes as Camille had. Danica's knees weakened; her pulse sped up. *Blake.* She wanted love, honesty, and Blake. Camille and Jeffrey kissed and the guests applauded, breaking through her reverie.

"I made a decision," Kaylie whispered.

Danica blew Blake a kiss from across the aisle and turned toward Kaylie. Her makeup barely concealed the dark circles beneath her eyes.

"I had a long talk with Chaz last night. We were up till dawn," she said.

"And?" Danica didn't know if she should hope they were going to have the baby or not. She only wanted Kaylie to be happy, and she knew Kaylie possessed enough love to be a wonderful mother, even if she was scared shitless. She also knew her sister well enough to know that once she made up her mind, there would be no turning back. Ever. She reached for Kaylie's hand as Camille and Jeffrey walked down the aisle, hand-in-hand, ducking under the flower petals the groomsmen threw above them.

"I love him," she whispered.

Danica leaned in closer. "You love him?"

Kaylie looked her in the eye and said, "I love him! I do! I really, truly love him!"

The church became quiet, like everyone held their breath at the same time, and all eyes turned toward Kaylie. She covered her mouth, her cheeks on fire. Kaylie turned toward the guests, looking like a kid caught with her hand in a candy jar. She mouthed, "Sorry," and wrinkled her nose.

A hearty, sisterly laugh escaped Danica's lips. She grabbed Kaylie and hugged her tight. "I'm gonna be an auntie!"

"Don't squeeze so tight. I'm feeling a little nauseous these days."

"Okay, sorry, sorry!" Danica hugged her again gently. She took Kaylie by the shoulders and looked seriously into her eyes. She searched for worry, discontent, something to indicate there might be trouble brewing, but for the first time in as long as she could remember, her sister looked content. "You're sure?" The therapist in her had to ask.

"One hundred and ten percent." Kaylie smirked. "Besides, if I flip out or something, I know this great therapist."

"No, by then that great therapist will be a youth center director, but she'll be able to refer you to a great therapist."

Blake waited for her in the aisle. Danica wrapped her hand inside Blake's arm and they fell into line behind the other bridesmaids and headed toward the reception room.

Blake leaned in close and whispered, "I never want to be away from you for that long again."

The End

Please enjoy the first chapter of the next
Love in Bloom novel

Sisters in Bloom

Snow Sisters, Book Two

Love in Bloom Series

Melissa Foster

INTERNATIONAL BESTSELLER

MELISSA FOSTER

Sisters in

Bloom

Snow Sisters

Chapter One

Kaylie Snow didn't just have to tinkle. She had to pee. If she wasn't out of bed in two minutes, she'd very likely not make it to the bathroom, and then she'd have to explain to her fiancé why the carpet was wet. She pulled the sheet over her naked, burgeoning belly and sat up, watching Chaz's chest rise and fall with each peaceful breath. She stifled the urge to lean over and kiss his barely parted lips. He'd been working so hard; he really did deserve to sleep in. The morning light streamed through the curtains, reminding her of the morning after they'd first met. Surely her bladder could wait one small minute while she savored those memories. She'd had far too many margaritas celebrating her best friend Camille's impending wedding, and Chaz had been only mildly tipsy when they'd left Bar None together and headed to his place. She remembered thinking that she wanted to run her hands through his wavy blond hair, which set off his ocean-blue eyes like jewels. And she'd desperately wanted to kiss him, just as she did now.

She'd waited a long time for that first kiss. They talked until five in the morning, when—tucked perfectly into the curve of his arm, her head against his muscular chest—they'd fallen asleep on the couch in his living room. When she awoke, the sun was warming the room, and his unkissed lips were slightly parted as he slept. She could feel their connection as if it were another person in the room, and she'd known in her heart that she'd found the man she'd one day marry. She reached over now and ran her finger over the prickles of whiskers that lined the chiseled edge of his jaw.

He rolled onto his side, snuggling deeper into the pillow, and shifted just enough to jiggle her bladder. She winced, pressing the heel of her hand on the mattress to push herself to her feet—not an easy task at thirty-five weeks pregnant. As she raised herself off the bed, she felt Chaz's hand fold into her own.

"Come back," he whispered.

Kaylie turned, holding the sheet across her heavy breasts. "I have to pee," she whispered.

"Then come back." He squeezed her hand gently and then let her go.

After Kaylie went to the bathroom, she washed her hands and inspected herself in the mirror. *Naked Buddha.* She turned sideways. *Beached whale.* She turned to the rear and looked over her shoulder. *Oh, God, that's even worse.* What had she been thinking last night, believing each of Chaz's compliments about how gorgeous she looked? The evening before came tumbling back to her. *The phone call from the Denver nightclub,* the one she'd sung in for the last two years. Just another in a long line of lost singing gigs that she'd hoped to secure for after the baby was born. She was a good singer! Audiences loved her, and she'd never missed a single gig. She'd always dreamed of being offered a record deal; now it seemed as if her pregnancy changed everything, like she had a tattoo on her forehead that read, *Don't hire me. I'll have a baby soon and it'll make me unreliable.* She'd cried for twenty minutes, blaming herself, the baby, and even Chaz. Later she realized she hadn't really meant a word of it; she'd just been overwhelmed. Chaz had stuck right beside her, calm and empathetic, and she'd fallen for every one of his lines about how sexy and beautiful she looked and how wonderful of a mother she'd be. He'd reeled her right into his loving, secure arms and whisked those worries away.

Look at me. That's it! No more sleeping naked. She ran her hands along the pockets of flesh that had somehow gathered above her waist. *Jesus, I have love handles?* She'd been a size five since she was a teenager. How could she have love handles? Babies grew in the uterus, not above the hip bones. *What the hell is this all about?* She patted her blond hair into submission—sort of—brushed her teeth, and then grabbed one of Chaz's T-shirts from his dresser drawer before returning to bed.

Kaylie lay on her back, her legs bent at the knees. She restrained herself from feeling the love handles that now seemed to silently taunt her. Just knowing they were there was making her cranky. She felt her chest tighten, and clenched her fingers around the edges of Chaz's shirt.

Chaz curled into her, his knees tucked under hers and his arm across her narrow hips, below her enormous belly. He rested his head on her shoulder, and she listened to his breathing, each breath calming her nerves a little bit more. She felt so safe when she was with Chaz. No wonder she hadn't put on clothes last night. She believed anything that came out of his mouth.

"Wanna think about names?" he whispered.

"We agreed not to." When Kaylie first learned she was pregnant, they'd decided not to find out the gender of the baby. There were so few real surprises in life that they wanted the birth of their baby to be one of those moments that really grabbed them by their hearts in a way that nothing else ever could. For that reason, and with her doctor's permission, she'd had only one sonogram. She wasn't a high-risk pregnancy, and she was so young that her doctor saw no reason to have more; Kaylie had been relieved. The idea of lying on the table with her baby on that screen—close enough to reach out and touch—would have been too hard to turn away from.

Kaylie was also adamant about not trying out names before it was born. She'd never understood how a child could have a name before the parents had met it. What if a Charles was really a Michael? It would be hard to change the name to fit the personality or looks of a baby if they'd been calling it Charles for nine months.

She and Chaz were so much alike. They agreed on almost everything, and Kaylie had dated enough men to know just how lucky she was. She closed her eyes, thinking about the things she had to do today. She was meeting her older sister, Danica, and her mother, whom she hadn't seen in—gosh—a year? Had it really been that long? Guilt settled in around her. Her mother was once such a big part of her life, but ever since she found out that her mother had stayed with her father after learning of his affair, she no longer saw her mother in the same light. The strong woman she thought she knew seemed weak and almost pathetic. Now that Kaylie was going to be a mother, she found herself thinking of her own mother more often, but she had no idea how to handle the anger and disappointment she felt toward her. Once again, she tucked away these uncomfortable thoughts about her mother. They were too difficult to deal with right then. She had other pressing issues that she could not ignore.

Her nerves tightened against the incessant nag in the back of her mind, the one that reminded her that it had been months since her last singing gig. The one that reminded her that her sister Danica would never let her career just fade away, unless that's what she wanted. Kaylie felt powerless to change the path of her failing career, and determined, fearless Kaylie had never felt powerless in her entire life.

Chaz moved his hand slowly across her pelvis, then traced gentle circles on the underside of her belly. "Gracie?"

"We're not doing this," she said, smiling despite her desire to chew on her worry for just another minute or two. She brushed his bangs from his forehead.

"Felix?"

"Chaz."

He scooted up beside her and whispered in her ear, "Jezebel? Bambi?"

She giggled. The stress of her love handles and the nagging were fading.

He nuzzled against her neck, bringing his hand over the crest of her belly, and then dragged his index finger straight down from her collarbone, between her breasts, to the arch where her belly joined her diaphragm. Shivers tickled her spine. She folded her legs to the side, leaning them against his.

"I'm meeting my mom and Danica for lunch."

"Mm-hmm." He kissed her shoulder, slipping his hands beneath her T-shirt.

"I haven't seen Mom in ages. I'm kinda nervous."

He slid the shirt over her head, and she arched as he pulled it off, her hair showering down around her face.

"Don't be," he said. Then he was on his knees beside her, one arm on either side of her body.

She traced a vein running over his biceps as he lowered his mouth to her breast. She gasped as he flicked her nipple with his tongue. Pregnancy had heightened her senses, and Chaz played into them with tantalizing care. She laid her head back, arching her neck, trying to hold on to her concentration, think through the impending meeting with her mother and her career troubles. But he shifted to the other breast, exposing her wet nipple to the cool air, and she grabbed the back of his head with a wanting moan.

Chaz ran his tongue along the outside of her breast. "Want me to stop?" He lifted her breast and lapped at the delicate skin beneath.

"No," she said breathlessly. Her hormones had been on overdrive since her fourth month of pregnancy.

His mouth trailed her side, her ribs, and then the area just above her hip.

She guided him back up, away from those newly formed love handles, and drew his mouth to hers, opening to him as his tongue moved slow and deep, exploring her, consuming her. She felt his hardness against her leg, and she pressed into him. His hand dropped to her other hip, sinking his fingers into the flesh of her thigh. Every nerve ending flamed with heat. She arched into him, her belly an unforgiving guard between them.

She sat up, and he moved with practiced care onto his back. Tension from the lost gig eased as his hands reached for her hips and she straddled him, hovering just above the tip of his desire. He arched toward her, and a sly grin spread across her lips. This had become her favorite part of pregnant lovemaking— taking control, making him wait. She leaned forward, her hair circling their faces, and she kissed him gently on his forehead, his cheek, his chin. Chaz tried to catch her lips with his, but she was too quick. She took his hands in hers and secured them under her knees, and then she leaned into him again, gently licking the edges of his lips.

She lifted her body higher, then pressed his erection flat against his belly, lowering herself onto him, teasing him, not allowing him to enter her. She glided up and down along him until his eyes were so full of hunger that she thought he might beg her for more. She relished in controlling his release. She kissed his chin, his neck, and then sucked just below his ear, until she knew he couldn't hold out much longer. She ran her tongue down his chest, taking his nipple into her mouth and using her teeth ever so lightly while he writhed beneath her, begging for her to take him inside. Finally, breathless with her own desire, she reached between her legs and guided him into her, sucking in air with the shock of him.

He opened his eyes and pulled her into a deep kiss. Kaylie felt the worry about seeing her mother ease from her shoulders and back. His hands slid down her sides, and she flinched, searching his gaze for hints of disgust from the thickness of her expanding waistline. She watched his eyes fill with desire and then flutter closed as he melted into the feel of her. She relaxed into his touch, her worry disappearing with each sensuous movement, until her self-consciousness, and thoughts of her wavering career, were almost—almost—gone.

To continue reading, be sure to pick up the next
LOVE IN BLOOM RELEASE:

SISTERS IN BLOOM, *Snow Sisters*, *Book Two*
Expected publication date October 9, 2013

Acknowledgments

Writing *Sisters in Love* has been a wonderful experience for me, and I've become tremendously attached to the characters, which means that readers can look forward to many more *Love in Bloom* novels. First and foremost, I'd like to thank my readers. You inspire me to dig deeper and reach further to bring you a variety of books with characters that remain with you long after you've read the last words.

I am blessed to work with a fantastic editorial team: Kristen Weber has not only been a constant in my writing life, but she is always available for guidance, advice, and support. Kristen, your friendship, editorial skills, and your willingness to push me to give my readers more are only part of what make you a true gem, and I am so thankful to be among your clients. Penina Lopez, you are as meticulous as you are professional, and without your efforts my book would be filled with homonyms and my readers would not be pleased. I'm grateful for your time, energy, advice, and guidance. Colleen Albert, you are so much more than a top-notch editor. You are a friend and colleague, and your support means the world to me. Thank you.

There are certain people who have spent countless hours listening to me gush over character crushes and worry over details. You've pushed, pulled, coddled, teased, and set me straight too many times to count. Each of you is my daily lifeblood: Hilde Alter, I could not have written a damn thing without having been your daughter. You've always believed in me, and you made me believe in myself. Thank you. Kathleen Shoop, you and I have grown up together in this publishing world. Thank you for your wisdom and your friendship. Stacy Eaton, Amy Manemann, Emerald Barnes, Clare (Rachelle) Ayala, Bonnie Trachtenberg, Wendy Young, Christine Cunningham, G. E. Johnson, and Natasha

Brown, aka Sis, not only do I know that each of you has my back, but you keep me sane, and I treasure our little family. Russell Blake, you never fail to make me laugh, you provide a basis for competition, and you push me past my boundaries, but mostly, you just *get it*. You're a hell of a writer and a hell of a friend. Thank you.

I'm a social media addict, and I appreciate each of my friends and fans for indulging me, encouraging me, and inspiring me on Facebook and Twitter. I look forward to our chats and jokes, and I am so thankful for each of you.

Regina Starace, thank you for creating the perfect cover for this book. I am honored to work with you. Jane Porter, it means the world to me that you read and enjoyed Sisters in Love. Thank you for your generosity. Kian Vencill, Pat Fordyce, Deb Shanley, and Kathie Shoop, thank you for reading early versions of this book, for providing valuable feedback, and for your unrelenting friendship and your support.

No author writes alone, and no author succeeds alone. I am blessed to have a tremendous support team of writers, bloggers, and readers. Team PIF (Team Pay-It-Forward) is the best damn street team around, and I adore each and every one of you. You're talented, generous, and you never fail to make me smile. Thank you.

I am married to the best man on the planet. Hands down, he is the most supportive, loving, generous, intelligent, and patient man I know, not to mention he makes me laugh night and day. Les, you never complain when I'm locked away with my keyboard, or when I tell you I've fallen in love with another fictional man. You laughed when I started writing romance and I asked you to start wooing me like fictional heroes do—and then you did it. You own my heart and soul, and I adore you.

Thank you for supporting my dreams and for sharing my life.

No one feels the brunt of my crazy hours like my children do. They eat takeout more than they should, and they laugh at me when my characters make me angry. Here's to you, kids. I love you all.

Melissa Foster is an award-winning, International bestselling author. Her books have been recommended by USA Today's book blog, Hagerstown Magazine, The Patriot, and several other print venues. She is the founder of the Women's Nest, a social and support community for women, and the World Literary Café. When she's not writing, Melissa helps authors navigate the publishing industry through her author training programs on Fostering Success. Melissa hosts Aspiring Authors contests for children, and has painted and donated several murals to The Hospital for Sick Children in Washington, DC.

Visit Melissa on her website, chat with her on The Women's Nest, or social media. Melissa enjoys discussing her books with book clubs and reader groups, and welcomes an invitation to your event.

Melissa's books are available on Amazon.

www.MelissaFoster.com